SAFE HAVEN:
Warrior Chronicles
The Coming Storm
Caitlin Andrews

This novel was written and completed for the National Novel Writing Month (NaNoWriMo) challenge, an international competition in which hundreds of thousands of writers participate annually.

Out of the 310,000 writers who attempted this feat, Andrews was one of 42,000 (14%) to actually complete the challenge.

The bulk of this book's contents was written in November 2013, and has been refined for the readership of the general public.

To my sweet family:
Mom, Dad and Dan, you have always
been my greatest support, my heroes.

And to Tiffany and Naomi, for
imagining with me through the years,
being the best friends a girl could have.

Prologue

Over the high crested mountains and snow-capped peaks, rock aged with weather and time, stands an ancient land. This land, belonging to a kind not unlike our own, is quiet, and wild, and alive. Beyond these mountains, a fine barrier of nature, lays the realm of a mysterious kind- older than the human race by several thousand years.

This is the land of the elves.

There is an unspoken law amongst humankind. None may ever pass over these mountains, none may witness the wonders that lie on the other side. Humans have long wondered and wished to know what lay hidden on the other side of the Petoac mountains, beyond the stone giants that reached toward the blue sky in tacit worship. But all knew better than to traverse that sacred path. The Goddess meant for her children to be divided- or so the humans told themselves. Something pulled humanity to the mountains, to see what lay beyond- but few ever dared to make the journey.

Few who attempted this quest ever returned. The road was long and rough; uncharted gullies and rivers cut through the land and wild woods stopped many in their travels. Those who managed to return to their small villages and worrying families spoke of a tower- a tall black tower. Nobody had gotten close enough to discern what exactly this structure meant, or why it was built into the side of the mountains. Who- or what- lived up in that lone keep? No one dared to approach the alien building, for many reported after seeing the tower that they began to hear voices in their heads. Grown men broke, claiming to have heard their dead mothers and wives, long lost by disease and war. And shimmering lights- they spoke of glowing spheres on a lake. These travelers were denounced, their visions declared to be lunacy. Priests warned that it was the Goddess commanding them to return home, that the land beyond the mountains was forbidden, ancient, and dark. Nonetheless, it told the world of man that there was indeed something beyond those rigid peaks; that their distant cousins wreathed in legend may exist.

Most of humanity remained ignorant to the world that lay to the east of the Petoac mountains. There were a few periphery villages in the mountains wreathed between the borders, but their existence was little known and their inhabitants rarely left the townships. Outside their walls lay the untamed wild, and not even the elves knew all the creatures that ruled that forest. The Petoac mountain range slopes down into the forest, rough and untamed. Leaves blot out the sun and allow for all manner of faerie and beast to glow their bioluminescent patterns. Blending with the natural hues of the wood, the faerie folk live aloof; concerned not for the weary traveler. Gnarled trees and dark canopies slowly give way to the plains, where wind whips across the rigid grass, and the Goddess's timeless melody is sung throughout the land. If one traveled far enough, they would eventually come upon the Sea of Glass, a crystalline body swathed with jagged cliffs and hot springs.

The world lies as it should, a beautiful haven for all the inhabitants who occupy her embrace. The elves, rulers of the faerie folk that dapple the landscape, live in unity with their land, learning from and caring for it. The elves call their blessed lot Eringoth. This realm was divided into four lands- the North, South, East, and Western kingdoms. Our tale begins in the proud Northern Kingdom, ruler of the other three lands and the central concentration of elfin life. Totally encompassed by the Royal Forrest, this kingdom is nestled in a nook of the Petoac Mountains, nearly hidden from the rest of the world. The oldest and most powerful of the Quartet Kingdoms, the North is ruled by the ancient Cendra family line. For hundreds of years, peace and prosperity have reigned in the land of Eringoth. There was no war, no famine- simply coexistence with the land.

There have been stirrings in the West, in the human world beyond the Petoac ridges. Elfin scouts have noted distress amongst the humans, moving toward preparing for battle. For what battle, no one could be sure. It was unknown for what humankind was preparing, and the elves, despite their aloof nature, began to take notice. Rolling over the mountainside was a cold chill laced with a thin veil of magic. Spring had come early that year, but the cold of winter had not yet waned. Thunderclouds churned on the daily, blotting out the setting sun and turning the canvas of the sky the hue of a dark rose. Sometimes it seemed like the sky was raining blood- but no one could be sure. The elves looked on passively at first, noting the ephemeral beauty in the red rain before returning to their simple lives.

But then, a few began to worry. Aged mages and wizened counselors to the king began to whisper in his ear. Nothing like this had happened before, in the texts of elfin lore no one had known what it meant to see the weather act so strangely. Nature meant everything to these creatures, and when one small element fell out of balance, the rest was sure to become compromised as well. It was the way of the world, and the elves listened to the Goddess speaking her truths through the skies and the ground.

The king, Lord Dromo Cendra, listened carefully. He, having a family of his own and all of Eringoth to look after, decided to call for his best knights. There would be covert preparations in case humankind became threatening, and to ensure that nothing else accompanied the strange weather. The elves looked to the sky and wondered. As the land would become veiled in a red haze nearly every afternoon, they looked to the West, over the land-barricade of mountains, and prayed to the Goddess.

One such child of the Great Mother would be particularly affected by the mysterious circumstances at hand. She belonged to neither side of the mountain, and felt a deep stirring of trouble in her heart when hearing of the anxious humans. On a particularly rosy afternoon, this young woman rose from her etiquette training, stalked from the room, and carried herself directly to the armory. Professors called for her to return, to finally start acting like a woman of court, but she was deaf to these pleas. Something deep in her chest was telling her to prepare. Something told her that a storm was coming.

One

KOHAN

A YOUNG GENTLEMAN lounged comfortably on a plush red chair, examining the blade of a finely crafted dagger. *So much to do, so little time*, the back of his mind whispered as he rubbed the hilt of the knife. A meeting with the Council of Elders, a lavish dinner with the family, and to round out the evening, a ball to commemorate the coming spring. Mid-afternoon light poured in through the stained glass windows, warping the colors of the drawing room into rich golds, greens and reds. The man became a silhouette to the light, the solitary flash of his blade cutting through the dim.

He grimaced, wishing he could skip the meeting and get on with the rest of the evening. All the Elders ever did was disagree with his father. It was the same every time- his father wanted to reform this law or that code- and all the Elders ever said was no. The man was beginning to think that they needed a different strategy. His mind wandered on to the good meal awaiting him that evening and, more importantly, which dance he had saved for what lady at the ball. It was tiring, having to satisfy so many fine ladies in one evening. A small smile swept onto his fair lips. Oh, how he loved the intelligent discourse and banter that ensued.

"Prince Kohan," a voice interjected from behind.

The subject addressed lolled his head backward and found an upside down messenger in his view. "Yes, master Sean," Kohan replied, hoisting himself up and stretching out his arms. Now was not the time to be thinking such leisurely thoughts. Re-sheathing his dagger, he said, "It's a little early to be calling me to the Council."

The small messenger shook his head. "It's the King, my lord. He wants you to meet him on the balcony." He stepped aside as Kohan strode by.

"Thank you, my good boy," Kohan grinned, tousling the page's hair. "See to it that my things are gathered for the dance later this evening."

"Yes, my lord." Sean grinned past his mussed hair and scurried down the corridor.

Kohan's maroon cape billowed behind his long stride down the castle hall. His boots clicked on the marble floor, shadow disappearing and reappearing as he stepped in and out of the light that streamed through the long windows. The prince's claret hair glowed in the mid-afternoon light- he dragged a hand through it, rounding a corner and arriving at the balcony. Overlooking the practice fields stood his father, clad in only robes of white silk. A red-stoned necklace that hung to his chest was the only trinket of value that the king bore. Kohan slowed his step upon entering his father's presence; he may be a prince, but his father was the true ruler.

"You wished to see me, my lord?" Kohan queried, standing tall and waiting for his father's reply.

King Dromo was silent for a while, his silver head bowed almost as if in prayer. A delicate crown of antlers and vines wove about his forehead; small white flowers sprinkled amongst the leaves gave the impression of little sprites dancing about his head. The king made no move to turn and greet his son- he seemed to be focused on something below on the grounds. His hands were thoughtfully knotted behind his back.

"Have a look at the knights below, my dear son," The king stated with a gesture to the greens. His gentle hand glazed over the landscape beneath them; the world seemed a little brighter after he passed over it. "And see if there is anything unusual that strikes your eye." His soft voice rolled over the balcony as a stream, gentle and powerful at the same time.

Kohan stepped in line with his father, feeling a rush of air caress his face as he neared the edge. He looked over at the soldiers, toiling in preparation for the uncertain future. Chain mail glinted as the warriors ducked and twirled around one another in the practice rings, swords flashing in sparks when contact was made. Next to the rings were the archery lanes- most were filled at this time- and Kohan's elfin ears picked up the distant sound of metal striking wooden targets. Tump. Tump. Tump. He recognized a few of his comrades amongst the training knights; smiles and salutations greeted the prince when they met his gaze. With a nod of his head and an open grin, Kohan continued his search. There were several crests that he didn't recognize.

"Those are knights hailing from the East," Kohan surmised, squinting at the symbols on the elfin armor. Many were in the forms of sea creatures, coastal birds and marshland dwellers. The knights all seemed fairly uniform, with dark weathered skin from the ocean sun and worn from defending their towns from all manner of thief, pirate and beast. "They arrived later than expected. And they seem quite weary." he gathered, noting the rather small quantity of their troupe and the traces of exhaustion on their faces.

Lord Dromo nodded knowingly. "The journey to the North was long. In the Royal Forrest they encountered a rampaging pack of wild boars and quite a few have been wounded." Kohan caught the King looking to the sky above the mountains, and the traces of red that dappled the grey clouds.

"The Forrest has been plagued with a manner of interesting sprites recently," Kohan said, recalling a conversation he had with some merchants that had just arrived in the North. One had spoken of being attacked by a horde of hostile faeries for plucking a single mushroom from the side of the road. Another mentioned the watchfulness of deer, bear and raccoon, and the sense of uneasiness about their oddly conscious gaze. "Do you know what it means?" The prince asked, looking beyond the castle walls and into the trees, dark claws under the sinking sun.

It was common knowledge that entering the Forrest was a danger- not even the elves knew of all that lived in the dark foliage. For the most part, however, the elves ignored the Forrest and the Forrest let the elves alone. It was odd to find so many attacks by relatively normal creatures on unsuspecting travelers.

"The land is restless," Dromo replied, following his son's gaze. "I can feel it. The ground shakes and the trees groan. But I do not yet understand why. Something deep in my heart is telling me that I need to discover it, and soon."

Kohan looked over at his father, surprised to find him with a deep worry in his eyes. King Dromo was an elf, a rather young one when looking at the age of the Council, but in that particular instant, to his son he seemed to carry many generations of worry. Kohan inhaled the afternoon air, taking in the wild scent of the woods and the fresh green earth. Kohan knew how much the land and this kingdom meant to his father. Having been its ruler for nearly thirty years, Dromo had weathered many a storm with his people. But this particular tempest seemed different than of those past.

Kohan rested a hand on his father's shoulder. "Do not be concerned, father," he began, "I shall do my part and question the new coming knights. Anything I find will be reported immediately back to you."

"Thank you, my son." Dromo glanced gratefully at the prince, pride twinkling in his light green eyes. "You may just yet be ready to fill my place one day." The King thought for a moment, glancing sideways at Kohan. "And I know that you will have no issues in finding a bride. In that arena you are already a true king."

Kohan's eyebrows lifted quizzically. He felt the first prickling of blush creeping to his face. Not knowing whether to laugh or quickly excuse himself, Kohan averted his eyes and found himself staring at the training grounds once more. And then- something else caught his eye, something that made him blink twice, for fear that his vision was deceiving him.

Off to the left by the ivy-chocked stone wall lay the jousting courts, where a small crowd of squires and fellow knights had gathered. A showdown was about to begin. The knight who had his back to the balcony was obviously foreign; his crest bore the insignia of a mallard duck and he had dark skin. He saddled up, facing a much smaller opponent clad in the standard Northern red armor. The breast plate was much too large and the helmet seemed to slump over the rider's eyes. The knight hoisted the javelin with strength but not with style; as he raised it high in the air, his fellow knights cheered uproariously. Kohan focused in on that Northern rider with disbelief, noting the raven back hair that spilled from under his helmet.

"My lord," Kohan began, gesturing to the event about to take place, half considering to clamber from the balcony to stop the challenge. "Is that—"

"Yes, it is." Dromo asserted, his lips curved into a slight smile. He had placed a firm hand on Kohan's arm- the prince resisted the urge to shirk away. He remained by the King's side as the ruler watched, lips drawn into a thin line, waiting for the event to unfold.

The majority of Kohan's friends rallied around the red knight, slapping him on the back and rearing him up for the charge. Several squires were fixing his armor and giving the knight pointers on how to properly hold the weapon. On the opposite side of the lane, the Eastern knight was joined by some of his comrades, and by the contortions of their faces it seemed to Kohan that they were yelling inflammatory remarks across the field. The mallard knight prepared for the charge, readying his shield and his javelin.

A neutral page on the center sideline hoisted up a red flag, and the lane fell silent. At this point, the rest of the trainees had stopped their drills, swords and bows slack, waiting for what was going to happen next. Long shadows stretched across the dirt path, striping the lane in light and darkness. The page waved his red flag and swept it downwards; a roar of enthusiasm ensued.

The mallard knight kicked off his large brown steed first, getting a jump start down the lane and charging his opponent. He anchored himself down low to his horse's neck, picking up speed and taking aim at his target. The red knight kicked off as well, but struggled with carrying both the sword and javelin, as they were quite heavy for him. He adjusted as he picked up speed, urging on his dapple grey.

It was obvious which opponent held more skill; waiting for the collision was hard for Kohan to bear. He gripped the balcony with white knuckles, wondering what in the world had brought on this confrontation. It was clear that it was more than just friendly jousting- there were some kind of stakes behind this battle. Honor was on the line here. Kohan knew he shouldn't be as surprised as he was.

The red knight bounced rather violently on his steed, unable to attach himself to the horse for support. They were almost to the middle now, javelins lowering, preparing for contact. The red knight's javelin made contact first, with the mallard warrior's shield. The javelin splintered on contact, bursting into thousands of tiny shards that littered the air, glowing in the setting sunlight. The red knight, thrown off balance and perturbed by the shower of splinters, was not prepared for the mallard knight's strike. He came down hard on the red knight's shield with extra force, and blew by his opponent, javelin intact. The mallard knight dealt a heavy blow; his shield arm was wrenched at an unnatural angle as he tumbled from his steed into the lane. Dirt and grass sprayed; the red knight lay immobile on the ground.

The red knight's comrades gathered around their fallen companion, asking of his health. They attempted to hoist their fallen friend, but the red knight rose of his own accord. Kohan involuntarily shuddered at the fall, wanting more than anything to go down to the fields and help.

"Not this time, my son." Dromo said knowingly, sensing the tension in Kohan's body. "This is her fight."

Kohan took heed of the stately voice and steeled himself, looking down as the confrontation unfolded.

The red knight stood, whipping off the too-large helmet in frustration and throwing it to the ground. Pulling the hair out of her eyes, Kohan caught the face of his little sister, flushed with anger and pain. He couldn't tell what she was saying, but knowing her, it was probably a stream of curses. The other knights were attempting with consoling words to convince her to back down, that she had tried and that was enough. The woman shook her head resolutely, and persisted to return to her mount.

Some of the knights shook their heads but remained by her side, adjusting the saddle and handing her a new spear as she reoriented herself on the dapple grey. She clutched at her shield arm, attempting to loosen it, but even from where Kohan stood he knew that it was in bad shape. The determination in her glare rooted the prince to his spot; he waited to see what she would do next.

The mallard knight rounded on his horse, muffled jeers pouring from his helmet. In response, the woman hoisted her javelin in challenge- she wanted to face him again. The Eastern knight fell silent for a moment, either bemused or intrigued. Wordlessly, he returned to his end of the lane and waited for the woman to do the same. The tension on the practice fields was rising noticeably now- the crowd had grown two-fold since the duel began- and now all waited breathlessly for the second round to begin.

The page hoisted the red flag once more, and with its fall the two knights were off to the charge again. With a cry the woman urged on her horse, her black mane of hair whipping all around her. From the start it was obvious that the shield was weighing her wounded arm down. She struggled to remain seated on her mount, but managed to latch on better than before. She leaned into her horse, urging him onward, pain and resolve plastered onto her face.

The mallard knight gave a cry as well, charging with great force into the middle. He lowered his spear and prepared for the second impact. A great gasp accompanied the red knight's charge- instead of raising her shield, with all the strength she could muster, the woman stood on her mount's stirrups and hurled her shield toward her opponent. The eastern knight's spear hit the shield at an angle, wrenching the red knight's weapon from his hands and forcing it down into the dirt. The mallard knight was leaning off of his mount- Kohan's sister seized the opportunity and launched her javelin forward. It hit the mallard knight's shield squarely in the center and he was sent hurtling backwards upon impact.

Dirt sprayed as the red knight rushed past. The very air seemed to cling to the moment, and all eyes moved from the fallen knight to the one still seated on her mount. Disbelief streaked across the woman's face, mouth agape at the crumpled knight on the ground. The Eastern elf's comrades rushed around him, shock and disappointment in their voices, trying to raise the man from unconsciousness.

The Northern knights looked around at one another, then to the woman, then to the neutral page who held the flag. The boy gestured with the pole toward the red knight, in affirmation of her triumph.

With a clear and proud elfin voice, one of the knights cried, "Victory, to the Princess Haven Cendra!"

An uproarious clamor ensued as the crowd surged around the princess's horse. She let herself be removed from the mount; apparently it was hard for her to stand. Through the exhaustion and the hurt, Haven stared up at the sky with an enormous grin.

Kohan let himself deflate when the fight was won, not knowing if he wanted to sweep his younger sister into a hug or scold her for her stubborn behavior. Nevertheless, he beamed at her from the balcony above, proud that victory had been hers. He looked over to the King, who was also watching his daughter, traces of contentment dancing in his eyes.

"Do you have any knowledge as to what this quarrel was all about?" Kohan asked, watching the Eastern knights pick up their disoriented comrade. He still seemed to be gurgling scathing remarks despite his confused state.

Dromo shook his head. "Although I know not the cause of this battle, I can well guess its roots. You know well the struggles my daughter faces, the discrimination that plagues her life. I can only guess it is yet another one of those confrontations." The king laced his fingers around a red crystal that hung about his neck, stroking the gem restlessly. It was a stone that had been given to him by his second wife, one that he never removed from his being.

Kohan exhaled, his brow creased in thought. He was well aware that his father was taking part of the blame for Haven's troubles. He also knew Haven would never want the King to be thinking this way. This was her fight, and her fight alone. Kohan could not persuade the king of this, however, and so the loyal prince stood by his father in silence, as they both thought on their beloved princess.

Down below in the training fields the crowd was beginning to disperse. Kohan saw the mallard knight-now mostly conscious-grudgingly shake hands with the princess in a duel well fought.

Haven's face was solemn, but there was an unmistakable confidence burning in her eyes.

Eventually, fellow Northern knights carted Haven off into the sick bay so that her wounds could be attended to. Her closest comrades remained by her side as the small troupe disappeared into the barracks. The king and prince remained on the balcony, watching as more thunderclouds began to roll in. The setting sun was a bloody orange slice in the sky, slowly being overtaken by the storm. Flecks of rain began to stain the stone walls of the castle and the scent of wet grass was rising from the fields.

"The time is nigh. We must meet the Council of Elders," Dromo declared, rising to his full height and turning to go inside. His silver hair glistened in the fast-waning light, the sun accenting his strong, angular face. To Kohan, the man looked tired, in need of a long rest.

"We had best be going then," Kohan fell into step with the king. "They will be more foul than usual if we aren't punctual."

The king smiled grimly. "An angry Council is the last problem we need. Come, Prince Kohan, let us go before the rain sets in."

The fields and the balcony emptied as the skies opened up. The Goddess rained down her tears on all the land; the Northern Kingdom fell silent under her wrath.

Two

HAVEN

THE WORLD WAS A BLUR. There were muffled sounds, a soft yellow light, and hushed voices, voices all around. The girl couldn't make sense of what was coming from where; she rubbed her eyes in attempt to gain some clarity.

"Goddess. She must have passed out," came a voice, seemingly from the left. It belonged to a younger man, perhaps a squire.

"It's her arm. That first joust combined with the fall, must have hit her harder than she let on," said another voice, more authoritative, hailing from the right. It must have been the squire's master.

They were both hushed by a nursemaid who had bustled near; Haven felt her arm and shoulder being prodded by soft fingers. In her half-dimmed vision she could make out the two men by her bed standing off to the side, watching the nurse set to work. The she-elf was clad in simple garments- a soft maroon cotton dress and a white working apron. Her hands worked deftly, using her many years of medicine to help discern the problem.

Haven heard a sharp exhale, and the sound of clinking medicine bottles. "It's this right shoulder, there's no doubt about that," The nurse clucked her tongue, continuing her examination. Haven felt a spark of fire when the woman pressed near her shoulder; she groaned and tried to pull away. "Not so fast, your highness. I'm afraid you've sprained it. You'll have to lie still for me," Next came the pungent scent of a magical balm.

Haven blinked and attempted to gain a bearing on her surroundings. She gathered she was in the sick bay, judging by the large open windows and dull roar of the waterfall that was known to exist just outside the medical area. The room had darkened under the wrath of the storm outside; rain spit on the windows and ran down the glass in a lucid red. Candles had been lit all around the work site, and the entire space glowed in a soothing light. Haven knew she didn't have time to waste here, and certainly wasn't looking forward to any potential treatment she might receive.

Still half-conscious and becoming moodier by the second, Haven tried to sit up- she was forced back down by the two men. "Fintan—Sir Gideon—what are you-" she struggled with her words and the arms that were holding her down.

"We're well aware you hate these procedures, princess," the younger boy-Fintan- started. "But ye have to lie still, please." Through her muddled vision Haven could make out the concern in the squire's face, his wide blue eyes gazing intently at her. Traces of manhood were accompanied by his dropping voice and sharpening face.

"This is your fault, if you think about it," Gideon stated bluntly, his head dipping to one side as he eyed her. "You could have walked away and saved yourself all of this trouble." Dimples and a white grin greeted Haven from his chiseled face. Choppy, uneven russet hair fell into his dark eyes. The knight still wore his uniform's undershirt, half untucked from his black pants. A belt clung to his waist, accented with his favorite dagger and other assorted trinkets.

"You know I couldn't have done that, Gideon," Haven grunted, slacking her limbs in defeat. The nurse frowned at the tall knight, wordlessly ordering him to move, and was at Haven's side once more. Prior to Haven's return to semi-consciousness, her armor and chain mail had been removed. Now the nurse rolled up Haven's sleeve and began to apply a congealed liquid to her bruised flesh.

Haven shut her eyes, hoping to also close out the pain. She felt Gideon's large hand on her forehead. His voice was a little softer than it was before. "It will be over soon. It's not as bad as you think."

Haven was grateful for his encouragement- this was the first time in a long while that she had required magical treatment to heal a wound. The last serious time Haven needed such aid was as a child, when Kohan had badly pranked his little sister and she fell out of a tree, dislocating her knee. There had been countless occasions on which she would need a magic balm to heal cuts and bruises, but on-site healing was a concern for her. Magic in general intimidated the girl- it wasn't something she possessed herself, and was afraid of its power. She preferred her battles to be fought on the exterior, not within with the aid of alien forces.

"Not to worry, your highness, I've done this procedure on many a wounded knight- some of whom are standing in this room," she shot a glare at Gideon, who shook his head with a smile. "Although there are a few differences in your physical composition, everything should run smoothly. Your human handicap shouldn't effect the process."

Haven's eyes hardened at the nurse's casual reference to her "composition"; she turned away to refrain from saying anything inflammatory. Fintan and Gideon exchanged a knowing glance; the former looked down to his feet with balled fists and the knight crossed his large arms, lips in a firm line. They stood at odds to the nurse at work; Gideon looked as if he wanted to confront the woman head-on.

Fintan fortunately gathered this response from his master and held out an arm, barring his path. He shook his head and murmured, "It's best not to get involved. Milady needs this treatment and she's already had enough to worry about today. Let it go," he pressed, easing the knight backwards.

Haven caught Gideon muttering about how the princess deserved more respect from a petty nursemaid, but he stood down and retreated back with his squire. Their eyes locked for a moment and understanding passed between them.

While she didn't outwardly express it, the princess was incredibly grateful for their inaudible support. The Northern knights and warriors-to-be were part of a handful of elves in the kingdom that respected Haven as both a princess and as a person. It hadn't always been that way- she had to prove her worthiness to them through her cunning and strength in battle just as she would with anything else. But the scholars and bureaucrats of the court who would quite patiently view Haven's academic, courtly, and political interactions with aloof faces and disappointed voices, would claim that she could not find a place in the palace.

It didn't matter how hard Haven tried- because she was half human, she could simply never succeed as an elf would. However, when she demonstrated her talents to the Northern warriors, they found her human intuition to be inspiring and fascinating. She earned respect amongst them and eventually, despite her being both half human and a woman, became considered a kinsman to them. It didn't matter that human blood ran in her veins- she was a strong and determined soldier- and that was all the knights cared about. So there they stood, two of Haven's closest comrades, supporting her in such a manner that few elves would. One day, she hoped to find the right words to express her thanks to them.

The nurse caught naught of this interaction between the knight and his squire- or she chose to ignore it- for she set straight to work on Haven's arm.

"Let's just get this over with so I can start the rest of this lovely evening," Haven snorted, her voice laced with sarcasm.

Large dinners and ceremonies were never of her liking- and the Goddess's Spring Revival was no exception. Not only did she have to wear confining gowns and act properly, but it was as if she was on a podium for all to stare at in wonder. The people of the court in general were nice enough, but Haven knew there was a never-ending stream of commentary about her trickling behind closed doors.

Fintan approached the wounded warrior, gently placing a wet rag on her forehead. "You can always come to the kitchen and visit me," he attempted to console her, his adolescent smile brightening Haven's spirits a little. "I would be honored to have your company,"

"The kitchen is no place for a princess, young master Fintan," The nurse interjected, finishing her lotion work on Haven's shoulder. The girl winced as the balm seeped into her flesh. "Besides, I hear the Eastern knights and scholars will be joining the feast. It should be an eventful evening, to say the least."

Haven said not a word, steeling herself for the night ahead and the surgery at hand. "Step back if you please, masters," the nurse said, holding out her arm and fixing her flaxen white hair. Her light eyes and pale face held an angel's likeness in Haven's confused vision. "You'll be just fine, my lady," she cooed, sensing Haven's unease. "Now all you have to do is breathe; leave the rest to me."

The princess closed her eyes and forced out a breath. Her jaw clenched tight and her fists were rigid rocks. Breathe in, and out. Inhale, exhale. She could feel the comforting presence of her friends nearby, which helped to calm her nerves.

There was darkness behind Haven's eyelids as the seconds passed, but as she waited, a soft white glow illuminated the right side of her world. She knew that the nurse was making the necessary hand gestures, giving thanks to the Goddess with every stroke in the air. Next came the soft incantations, spoken in the

Ancient Tongue, praising the natural order of the body and asking for the strength to return that balance to the vessel at hand. Haven concentrated on her breathing, nervously anticipating the next phase of the healing.

There it was: first contact. As the nurse's fingers touched down, Haven's body immediately tensed. Warm lightning seemed to race across her shoulder and seep into her skin, whirring and jarring the inside of Haven's flesh. She could feel the magic bonding to her physical self, and for a few intense moments the pain was magnified enormously. Haven bit back the urge to scream.

"Don't come near her," The nurse warned quietly, her voice soft and focused. It seemed as if one of the two soldiers had attempted to step forward and comfort their friend. "We don't want an imbalance at this time with all of this magic inside of her body. Her vessel is weak and may not be able to handle the stress if I make a mistake." This was certainly no comfort to the patient.

The healing began. Haven forced herself to lie still; she could feel the glow around her wound intensifying as the magic led her tendons back to one another. There was a disconcerting noise emanating from her shoulder, like a thick rope was being wound very tight. Haven bit her lip as the tension increased. The incantations continued; the girl focused completely on her inner strength. She had done this before, she could do it again. *If I can joust a cocky quacking knight from the East, I can most certainly handle this.*

Suddenly, the tension dispersed, and Haven could feel a draining of sorts from her right side. The glow dimmed and the nurse ceased her chanting, withdrawing her touch from the princess. Haven sighed with great relief, despite feeling sapped of all her strength. It took a great effort to re-open her eyes. Her shoulder had gone numb, but the swelling had decreased and the bruises had faded to a soft pink.

"Now, it takes your kind longer to heal than it does for us," The nurse began. She took a roll of bandages and began to dress the wound. "And this phase in the healing is very fragile. If you overuse your arm and damage it further, you will need to return for more healing. Is that understood, my lady?"

Haven drowsily nodded her head, too tired to care about the remarks that would otherwise set her off. She let herself be coaxed into a sling.

"Look at that. You didn't die. Happy now, princess?" Gideon approached the patient as the nurse retreated to find a balm for Haven to take with her.

"I may have to challenge you to a duel if you persist in talking like that, Sir Gideon," Haven mumbled, a lopsided smile on her disoriented face. She allowed squire and knight to support her, one on each side. They eased her off of the bed and helped her to stand.

"I would be honored to accept such a challenge, my Lady," Gideon bowed his head in mock ceremony.

"My bet is on the princess," Fintan piped up from Haven's left, an impish look on his freckled face, to which Gideon laughed openly.

"The support is greatly appreciated, my loyal Fintan. I would expect nothing less of you." The knight piped back, thoroughly amused.

The nurse returned with a small green bowl with leather wrapped around the opening. "And young loyal Fintan, you are charged with the princess's medicine. See to it that it arrives to her bed chamber." She ordered, handing the bowl to the squire. She turned to Haven and inspected her handiwork. "Apply the balm twice a day, and Goddess willing, you won't have to see me for a long time," her voice relaxed, and her eyes met with Haven's deep emerald ones. "Try and stay out of trouble, okay lassie?"

Before Haven could even muster a reply, Fintan stepped in for her. "There are no promises, knowing her highness and that temper of hers."

"But we shall certainly keep two eyes on her, one for each of us," Gideon interjected, hoisting Haven on his hip, turning her face so that she could see his. "No more brawls with our Eastern guests. Can you do that, princess?"

"Even if I wished to, I'm afraid my strength is quite lacking to be doing anything of the sort for a while," Haven admitted as the three made their way to the door. She was a tad embarrassed, having to be lugged around in such a manner, but she was too tired to protest.

Thunder rolled through the walls of the sick bay, jarring everyone as they left the open-aired room for the corridor. The sun had completely set at this point, and the walls were lit with numerous torches and candles, their light dancing off of the marble floors and columns.

To Haven's immense surprise, upon exiting the sick bay, she found another dozen or so knights sitting, relaxing, chatting to one another right outside the doors. She recognized many of them to be her close friends, to she and Kohan both. They appeared to be waiting for her emergence from healing. When she and the two other men appeared, they ceased their personal conversations and broke into applause. Half-dazed, but thoroughly flattered, Haven couldn't contain her modest laughter.

Gideon looked down at his friend, smiling gently. "The rest of my troupe gathered outside here. Seems that everyone wanted to make sure you were okay." Speechless, Haven merely stared at the assembly of her comrades. To the other knights, Gideon called, "Everyone, the Queen of Jousting lives!" He hoisted Haven's good arm into the air. A cheer rose around them as their fellow knights came to greet Haven and their captain. A slew of words flew at her in congratulations.

"Not bad, lassie, being your first time in the joust," cried a blonde knight.

"With a little training on a mount and proper execution, you'll easily be one of the best riders in no time," said another, whose knowledge in such areas of battle was keen.

"Mister fancy-britches from the shores sure didn't know what hit him!" A round of laughter followed the last remark. Claps on the back ensured, and many hands were shaken. Haven felt herself turning beet red. She wasn't used to such high praise, or positive remarks in general, so she remained silent, accepting the compliments given.

"Very well done indeed, Princess Haven," A chilling, mocking voice cut through the warm congratulations. The corridor fell silent; everyone turned and looked down to see a tall figure clad in dark grey. That hall been empty no more than a few minutes before.

The knights straightened and hoisted their chins up, eyes turning to stone. Haven gestured to her friends to let her stand on her own; Gideon and Fintan backed away accordingly. The figure began to stride down the hall, an air of authority striking the ground with every step he took. Haven eyed the man suspiciously, rising to her full height as he came into the torchlight.

Standing a full two heads taller than the half-human, the man held an imposing aura over the hall. His robes, though grey in color, were richly decorated with inscriptions of the Ancient Tongue and shimmered in the yellow light. The color of his garments matched the color of his wiry hair, braided in traditional Northern knots. He wore a bright green ring with a silver gem at its center- a symbol that he was a member of the Council of Elders.

"I didn't have the pleasure of watching you claim victory this afternoon," He began, his low, undulating voice openly contradicting his words. "But I must say I'm rather surprised. I was unaware that our famed Northern Knights allowed a woman to fight their battles for them."

This remark solicited deep, penetrating glares from the knights that surrounded Haven. The princess set her jaw and looked straight into the man's eyes. "Councilman Unus," she started evenly, "I'm afraid you've been misinformed. I challenged the Mallard Knight on my own terms. He impugned my royal blood and dishonored my family. It was a matter of rectitude on which I was forced to act."

The men around her murmured in agreement, but upon receiving a sharp stare from Unus, they fell silent once more. Knights were below the Council in terms of rank. Haven was on her own with this one.

"If you're speaking on the matter of your inferior birth, I'm afraid no matter of savage battling can justify that," The Councilman retorted coolly, folding his arms in an air of superiority. "From whence you came, princess, there is no honor."

It felt as if someone had just punched Haven in the gut. Her face became flushed with indignation; it felt as if her blood was boiling. "You are out of line, Unus," Haven growled through gritted teeth, feeling every muscle in her body tense up. "I hope you repent those words, before I come after you with a spear."

"Tut, tut," The Elder admonished her, waggling a spindly finger in her face. "Threatening one of the Council? That human temper of yours is certainly a vile one. It may get you into trouble one day." This time Haven took a deliberate step toward Unus; the very air around her seemed to shimmer red. Councilman Unus adopted an amused smirk; it spread across his peaked ancient face like a crack in the desert.

"It would be wise of you to use those years of intuition to know when to back down, revered Councilman," Haven rumbled, attempting to see past her blind rage. For some reason, her hands seemed to be burning hot. Perhaps it was the perspiration under her gauntlets. The knights around her shifted restlessly, wary of both the authority in their presence and the struggle of their friend.

"On the contrary, princess, I believe it is you who must back down. It is time to stop playing these games, attempting to prove your worth to your kingdom." It was the Elder's turn to advance. His presence covered the smaller woman in shadow. "It is difficult to do so when there is nothing for you to prove in the first place."

The princess was visibly quivering. It took everything in her power to refrain from cursing at the infuriatingly calm elf in front of her. Haven sensed movement from behind; she turned to find Sir Gideon breaking ranks to stand in front of her.

"That is enough," Gideon interrupted, confronting the Elder before him. Unus seemed taken aback, his composure broken for the first time. He stood, fixed on the younger and more built elf before him. "I understand and respect your position as an Elder, my lord," Gideon began tensely, "but this is no way to treat the princess of Eringoth. She demands more respect than this."

It took a moment for Unus to regain control. Soon enough his sickening smirk had returned. "This is touching. The knight protects his princess. It is a shame, having to report the Captain of the Guard for stepping out of line."

"Report? What is going on here?" A new voice carried from further down the hall.

Everyone turned to find the prince of Eringoth staring quizzically at the scene unfolding in front of him. A stack of papers were in his grasp; he was in the midst of leafing through them when he rounded the corner, on his way to see his little sister at the sick bay. He had already prepared for the feast that was to take place that evening, and his ceremonial armor glinted in the candlelight. The future king was a sight to behold, and his presence certainly commanded the attention of everyone present.

Haven's flush turned to burning shame when her eyes met her brother's. This was the last situation on earth she wanted him to see. For all the times he had stood up for her, here she was again, making more messes for him to clean up. Kohan's questioning eyes shifted to meet with Unus's cold glare. Despite the Elder's refined countenance, his eyes shifted in mild apprehension. It was one thing to torment a half-human woman- it was a completely different matter to do it and be caught red-handed by the prince himself.

Unus turned to the prince with a flourish of his robe- Haven was almost positive that his garments slapped her legs on purpose- and faced Kohan squarely. "Your Captain is out of line," Unus declared, gesturing to the brunette elf behind him. "It is immensely disrespectful to be addressed in such a manner by a knight."

"There is a purpose behind everything my Captain does," Kohan asserted, stepping closer to the gathered group. His very presence in the area seemed to diffuse the tension that stifled the air. As he drew near, Haven could make out the familiar features on his face- his perfect, thin nose that slightly arched up at the end, his defined cheekbones and sharp jaw, the soft pink lips that were now curved in a disgruntled frown, and his eyes- hard and determined- glowed a dynamic maroon in the evening light.

Sometimes the court whispered about the prince's eyes- that he was cursed by a witch as a child and that his off-colored irises were a by-product of the spell. No one, not even Haven, was sure of why he looked this way. But one could certainly tell that his eyes commanded attention- whether that be flirtatious or authoritative.

Right now, those eyes were locked on Unus, and they were noticeably putting the older elf on edge. "Some sort of provocation must have taken place. For no other reason my Captain and knights would be so up-in-arms," Kohan continued, taking a sweeping glance at the other soldiers in the area, who were even by elfin standards, disgruntled. "I'm curious as to why you're even down near the sick bay, my lord," he pressed, suspicion glimmering on his countenance. He glanced at Haven again, taking in her emotional state which was betrayed for all to see.

Unus, despite his discomfort at the authority before him, seemed too duplicitous to make his intentions clear to the prince. "I heard rumor that an infection was spreading. I merely visited to assess and contain the situation," he replied fiendishly, allowing a twisted grin to crawl onto his face, in spite of himself.

Haven had been staring at the ground, humiliation wrapping itself around her like a cloak. She kept her head down despite the continued prodding of the Councilman. Pulling Haven from her own confrontations was the last thing that Kohan needed to be worrying about. She wanted to prove to him that she could handle herself in such scenarios. "Brother, I can explain-" she began.

"I think I understand perfectly well what is happening here," Kohan interrupted, stuffing his papers in a back pocket and confronting Unus head-on. "My good sir, it appears that I have just a dash of time in between my duties to discuss this infection with you. I can answer any questions you may have if you follow me." With a dismissive wave of his hand, Kohan gestured that Unus accompany him down the hallway, back from whence he came.

The Elder glowered down at Kohan as if he were viewing an itch he had to scratch, but assented to the veiled order with a smirk. "As you wish, your highness," Unus conceded. He turned one last time to face Haven, and with a curt nod he said, "Here's to a job well done, Princess."

With a guiding hand on the Elder's back, Kohan led Unus down the hallway. In a backward glance, Kohan shot an apologetic look to Haven. He really had wanted to commend her on the afternoon's victory. With a quick nod at Gideon, the prince rounded a corner and was gone.

When the two powerful men had left their presence, the remaining knights deflated, sighing with relief. There was a flurry of low remarks about the Councilman and more claps on Haven's back. With the banquet and ball to prepare for that evening, however, one by one the knights bid farewell and broke away from the crowd.

Haven was so flustered, overcome with anger and shame that she had to step away from everyone else. Leaning on a wall with her good forearm, she hid her eyes. She focused on her breathing and attempted to return it to normal. Decompress. The girl wanted nothing else but to crawl into her bed and sleep. No feast, no more people, no more Unus. From a little ways off, she could hear Gideon ordering Fintan to gather up and clean the rest of her belongings. Footsteps drew near her- she felt a familiar hand placed itself between her shoulders.

"I'm sorry, lassie." His voice was gruff; it was apparent Gideon wasn't used to counseling distressed women. "You shouldn't have to deal with the likes of him. I'm sure the Prince will get everything sorted out."

Haven wanted to protest, she wanted to round on her friend and stress that she wanted none of her burdens to fall on her brother. She wanted so badly to be able to stand up to Unus, to the Council, to everyone who demeaned her existence. But she knew if she said anything else that her temper would burst- and what would that prove? Everything that Unus said would be true. Her human emotions would ruin everything. She had to fight to remain calm. So in response to her friend's consolation, she managed a half-hearted thanks.

It was in that moment, leaning on the wall, that Haven first realized the condition of her gauntlets. Pulling away from the stone, she looked down at her hands. The material that covered the palms were ashy and warm. The slight scent of burned leather wafted to their noses. Gideon inhaled sharply. "What in the Goddess's name…" he trailed off, taking her hand in his. Gently, the Captain stripped off Haven's gauntlets, caring not to jostle her wounded shoulder.

Haven and Gideon both stared down at her bare hands. They were covered in the consistency of charcoal that was hot to the touch. Haven recoiled when brushing a finger along her skin. The remnants of small embers lay nestled in the black glowing a soft orange.

Haven looked at her friend, whose bewildered gaze matched her own. "Were you aware you had otherworldly gifts, princess?" he asked, unsure of what he was seeing.

The princess shook her head, open mouthed, not knowing exactly what to say. She closed her palm and the embers sparked into the air. The two watched as they sailed upward, little stars reflecting in the glass windows.

Gideon stroked her palm experimentally, eyes wide with wonder. An amazed smile sprouted across his face. "Unless you

placed your hands on a torch after we hauled you out of sick bay…
I believe it's safe to say that the Goddess has touched you tonight."

Three
AAREN

ON THE SAME STORMY EVENING, as the sun was closing in on her fusion with the earth, a great sorrow struck the land. In the mountains far to the West, a delicate rain began to kiss the forest canopy, leaving a cold wet mist to filter through to the ground. Droplets trickled down from leaves, weighing their little green spirits down until the burden was too great. A tall dark tower stood silhouetted in grey mist, its sharp stony face a contrast to the wild forest surrounding it. It stood on the periphery of the lands of Eringoth, watchfully observing the enchanted wood. A great chorused cry rose from this tower and the surrounding landscape- startled animals and birds flew from their nests; trees seemed to recoil from the mournful wail. A sadness bled into the land, for a great unnatural tragedy had struck the earth that nightfall.

The dying sun was blotted out by ominous clouds; the land was bathed in red. Rain dripped forth from the heavens, clear and pure, until it united with the ground. Clear water dripped into pools of mud, where it mixed with opaque blood. The red was diluted at the water's touch, and in small streams the mixture trickled down dirt paths, matting grass and flowing down, down the mountainside. White spheres flickered softly in the distance- indicating their home on the periphery of the lake. The blood, cloudy and curling hues of soft pink, met with this lake- a blooming flower beneath the surface of the water.

After the cries of anguish, the world was met with silence. The soft pattering of the steady rain was the only disturbance of the deathly chill that had begun to settle over the land. The sky was darkening, the veil of night beginning to shroud the atrocities that scattered the land under the sun that day.

It was in the woods due south that there was a stirring of life. A faint glimmer shifted amongst the gloom of the evening- a figure lay in the soft embrace of the earth. His white tunic was smeared with grime and red. The poignant scent of blood drifted from his side. From the path that the man had left behind him, it looked as if he had dragged himself quite a ways before collapsing from exhaustion. He lay still for many minutes; it was unclear whether he was attempting to regain his strength or if he had simply passed out.

The man felt a great heaviness on his eyes- it took everything in his being to open them to the darkening world around him. He groaned involuntarily, every muscle in his body burned with ache. His heart was beating uncomfortably fast; it felt as if it might burst from his chest. Grief wracked his being but no more tears would come. His lungs burned from the running, the yelling, sobbing. The sky was weeping for him now, the rain gently kissing the man's stained face. Upon forcing his eyelids open, the deep azure of his irises penetrated the grey world. He closed them again, wishing that he could wake up from this nightmare.

The man continued to lay in the rain until the numbness started to set in. His mind began to blur the horrific images of the day together until they were an indiscernible mass at the forefront of his vision. Faces smeared into one another, scenes of endless stairs, the lake down below, the ground running red. He closed his eyes to block out the screams that continued to echo in his ears.

A distant rumble of thunder startled the man from his reverie; the impact of the lightning shook the ground that he lay on and lit up the sky above. Beneath the nullified state that the man had willed himself into, a small voice cried that he needed to find shelter. He needed to get help. He could not waste away in the forest like this. There were things he still needed to do in this world- it was not the time to give into death's dark embrace. The man recoiled at this small clear voice. He wanted nothing more than to melt into the dark abyss, and forget.

If nothing else, Aaren, remember Harmony. The small voice cried, ringing in the man's ear. *Remember her.* That single thought struck the man lying in the grime, wiping away the cloud of delusion that surrounded him.

Getting up was the single hardest thing that Aaren ever had to do. He propped himself up on his elbows- streams of fire and pain seared up his arms. A similar reaction gripped his torso and legs. His head throbbed and the world spun when he tried to gain a bearing on his surroundings. The man fished around for a crutch of sorts- his hands landed on a steady stick. He tested it, thrusting the end into the ground, and then leaned all his weight on it in order to stand.

Aaren's physical self struggled with the strains of walking, but his mind was resolved. For a while, he limped down the small dirt path, not completely certain of the direction in which he was headed. He knew that if he stopped, however, that he would immediately collapse again. Aaren therefore focused on the immediate: finding a place to ride out the storm. The last thing he needed was to catch an illness- he was certainly susceptible to something of the sort in his anguished physical state. There were more things to be worried about than a cold out here in the wilds- Aaren kept a constant lookout in the shadows of the trees, well aware that something could be lurking close by. He used his sharp elfin hearing to pick up suspicious noises in the dim, and his bright blue eyes darted about, honing in on any sort of movement.

Luckily, the storm seemed to chase most creatures into their dens. Aaren did happen across a carcass dismembered beyond recognition and a restless herd of deer, but for the most part, the woods seemed benevolent enough to leave the wounded elf alone. After a time, Aaren came across a thicket that lay a little ways off the trail. He loomed closer to investigate, and found it to be an entrance to a small cave peeking out from the side of the mountain. Aaren's better judgment warned that this cave belonged to some sort of creature, but the elf was too exhausted to care. It seemed empty and unsuspecting enough, and the dryness of the interior was immensely inviting.

Aaren knelt at the entrance and crawled inside, the cuts on his palms reacting sharply to contact with the cool, hard stone. He propped himself up against the back wall so that the entrance was clearly visible and any trespassers could be spotted easily enough. It was at this time that Aaren could assess his wounds for the first time. He found numerous bruises and gashes along his arms and legs, but it was at his mid-section where he felt the most searing pain. Gently touching the right side of his ribcage, he located a serious slash wound- from the clean cut it made it seemed to be the work of a sword. He tried not to recall the recent memories that flashed before him when he felt the edge of the cut- the emotions he had tried to seal away were panging dully in his heart. Blood still flowed from the gash; the entire side of Aaren's tunic was stained the color of wine.

Aaren's hand traveled to his neck, where he felt the smoothness of an alien metal pressed up against his flesh. It took him a few moments to remember that it was a necklace, situated snugly against his throat. His fingers traveled along the unique design- small metal squares bound together by a tough thin wire. Each metal plate his finger brushed over seemed to be trying to break him as they clamped down on his skin. Experimentally, Aaren tried to find a way to remove the necklace but could find no end and no beginning to the chain; his efforts were in vain. This was the last straw. It was too much, too much. His walled mind broke and memories came lightning fast, flooding across his vision.

The day came back in hazy images. The earlier it was in the day, the brighter the memories were. Looking back on them now was like feeling poison ivy curling around his heart. Aaren remembered the sun glinting through the green foliage, riding with the Western royal hunting party. He recalled how brightly his sapphire armor reflected the sun's rays, mirroring the color of his eyes. There was banter and laughter- everyone looked forward to coming home after a good day in the forest.

But there was no good to come back to. The village was in utter chaos; Aaren recalled the ransacked houses, bodies littering the streets, and the screaming. So many cries of his people in torment. There were demonic creatures everywhere, monsters from the black pits of the earth whose evil was so great, they could not be named. He remembered the confusion and bewilderment as he and his party charged into the fray, fighting off the demons that ravaged his home. Then, looking to the tower. Feeling cold fear trickling down into his heart.

He charged forth, running up and up flights of stairs, his own horror his greatest strength. Down one hall, then another, reading the signs of destruction around him but constantly pleading to the Goddess that everything would be fine. Bursting down that final door- the last barrier- and that's when it all ended.

In that instant, everything was as vivid as when it had actually happened. Aaren recalled the familiar shadowy figure, the man that confronted him. One eye gleamed out at him from a shrouded hood. From his spiraling black robe he stood at the center, a dark angel ready to reap his harvest. A spidery grin seared across his pale cheeks. Aaren for a second time drowned in the ominous sense of dread that accompanied looking behind that man- the figures lumped on the cold hard floor.

Aaren pulled from this trance with a swoon. He slumped forward, not quite able to contain his distraught. He swiped at a tear that dared to roll down his cheek. Shoving the memories aside, he resolved to try and get some rest- his journey was far from over. Caring not to place too much pressure on his injured side, Aaren lay facing the entrance to the cave. Thunder rumbled outside, closer in proximity now, and lightning lit the mouth of the cave, streaking light into his world. For a moment, everything was illuminated- the vines curling down from the roof of the cave, the individual droplets falling from the heavens, and the wild forest that lay outside. As his eyes adjusted to the darkness, he found himself to be surrounded by moss that glowed unearthly pinks, purples and blues. He rested his head on a particularly plump mass of glowing fuchsia plants, the exhaustion of the day finally catching up with him.

In his drowsy state, he decided that the North would be his destination. It was a long journey, but it was one he took upon himself to take. The Crown needed to hear of this tragic day for the

Western Kingdom. Aaren feared that he was the only remaining soul who could tell the tale.

Four

HAVEN

THE PALACE of the Northern Kingdom stood out as a beacon of light in the young night. As the storm raged around the weather-worn walls, a brightness gleamed from the wide windows, striking the night with rays of yellow. From a distance, beyond the castle wall, the city's inhabitants looked up at the towering structure- it looked as if there were floating candles in the night sky, leading up to the house of the Goddess herself. A truly beautiful piece of architecture this castle was- every high-roofed hall and blue-tipped spire covered in ornate elfin carvings. Depictions of the natural beauties of Eringoth riddled the exterior of the castle. Crafted the land's finest artists, scenes of flower freckled fields, majestic waterfalls, all the land's Animalia, and great plains stretched over the expanse of the outside walls.

The Northern palace was the only such structure of its likeness in the land of Eringoth- elsewhere many of the elfin structures were smaller, and less reliant on the altering of materials from their natural state. Not even the elves are sure how the castle was created or if it was even of elfin origin. Some have said that humans helped with the construction of the palace; there are indeed many architectural similarities to the Northern castle and other human designs. Although no one is positive on who created the ancient structure, King Dromo had taken the liberty of enhancing its human features in attempt to bring about a sense of acceptance of the elves' cousin race. The king himself had imported finely crafted wooden furniture from the periphery towns in the Petoac Mountains to decorate his inner most chambers.

Dromo always wore human-made garments of silk or cotton, modest and unassuming for the dress of a king. The Council of Elders silently denounced this unofficial call to accept humanity. There was little they could actually do, for Dromo was artful with the manner in which he was integrating humanity into the elfin world. It was beyond the Council's jurisdiction when the king decided to hang human paintings and draperies in the halls of his own castle. But the Council always feared that more substantive action would be taken next, and that one day the king would threaten the elfin way of life for all of Eringoth.

There was a method to the king's almost subversive measures, as it was unheard of for a monarch to be so infatuated with humanity. Lord Dromo's second wife was human, and it was with this woman that he fell in love, and also sired his beloved daughter. Those who had known Dromo before he met Queen May would not have recognized the king of Eringoth. Dromo was not very different from the Council he now so heavily battled against in terms of elfin code and law. He was cold, proud and arrogant, much like Kohan's mother had been. Had he seen a half human woman living amongst the elves, he would have opted to eject her from his land. Elves who witnessed the transformation said that their ruler had been 'touched by humanity', that there was a power that May held over him that none could define. Many cursed her as a treacherous queen who turned their beloved ruler soft. They claimed he had been dominated by his emotions and lost sight of what was best for the realm.

Haven only recalled faint images of her famed mother, but knew deep in her heart from a very young age that she was a good woman. She would sit in rapture as her father told stories of his beautiful human queen, one who inspired hope and goodness and was fair to everyone, even though very few people were fair to her. Haven saw the sincerity in her father's eyes and believed every word.

The princess thought of her mother as she prepared for the trying evening that lay ahead, knowing that if May, as a full human, could withstand the judgment of the court, that so could she. Haven sat at her desk, eyeing the three-sided mirror and the reflections that each of them held. She wasn't particularly fond of what she was seeing.

The mass of black hair that always stood out in a sea of elfin blondes, whites and light browns, was piled meticulously on top of her head. Haven's maid had taken the time to place small pearls amidst the chaos- they glinted like small stars in the dead of night. Lip color brightened the girl's mouth and rouge had been padded onto her cheeks. Combined with smoky eye makeup and darkened eyebrows, the girl felt that her face weighed five pounds alone.

Her clothing was entirely another story. As if the corset that hugged her ribcage wasn't enough, Haven was requested by her father to wear an elegant and very expensive rose-colored gown. Upon hearing this request, Haven was more than a little shocked- Dromo knew how her manners were. It was a task in itself not to spill midmorning tea on her practice clothes. Haven's etiquette teacher was always scolding her for improper table manners, and just manner in general. The added burden of caring not to ruin a royal gown was not helping Haven's nerves.

Haven was told by her family and a few of her knightly comrades that she would look beautiful if she wasn't always so battle-worn. Tonight was no exception- the delicate mirage of her made-up figure was shattered by a newly dressed white sling that nursed her right shoulder. Thankfully Haven had managed to hide the burns on her palms with delicate silk gloves, but the fabric was irritating her skin. It wasn't particularly painful; Gideon had actually been surprised at how resilient Haven's hands had been to the mysterious embers. All that remained of the odd event was some ash and the girl's itchy skin.

Haven and Gideon didn't have much time to assess what exactly had happened down near the sick bay. All they really allowed themselves was a few more moments of pondering and taking in the shock itself. As Gideon was escorting the princess back to her quarters to be prepared for the coming evening, he had asked if she was okay.

"I'm a little unnerved for you. It's an odd day when you find flames spouting from your palms," Gideon found himself saying.

"They weren't flames, just embers," Haven corrected pointedly. No need to have the tall tales grow taller.

A shrug accompanied Gideon's sigh. "Do you think you will be okay tonight? It would be quite a shame if you caught your dress on fire." His tone indicated a jest, but Haven could tell he was being serious, too.

Haven felt fine after she descended from the height of her anger. After replying that she truly was okay, just tired, she caught him eyeing her from the side of her vision. She knew that he had every right to be worried, and she was mildly touched that the Captain was being so attentive. Being the only female warrior of the Northern knights made her somewhat of a treasure, and many of the knights had come to the habit of keeping an eye out for her.

Haven huffed a sigh into the mirror. More than anything else, she just wanted to smear her makeup away and go to sleep. But hunger gnawed at the inside of her stomach, and she knew that her comrades would be there to keep her company. And she hadn't seen Kohan much that day, other than their encounter in the corridor. Haven wanted to make it clear that she would take responsibility for any fuss that Unus was sure to stir up.

Steeling herself, Haven gathered her skirts and stood. If nothing else, she would make her brother and father proud tonight. Somewhere up in the heavens, Haven knew that her mother was watching, too. She made a quick prayer to the Goddess, asking for nothing to burn or stain her dress that evening.

Seeing as the storm continued to rage outside, the festivities were to be hosted indoors in the dining hall and ballroom, a magnificent conjoining space that was usually used for winter celebrations. Many were disappointed to hear that the merriment was to be made indoors, but complaints were quelled when one looked out onto the storm that continued to wrack the castle.

Haven was to be presented to the court that evening on the arm of another one of her comrades, Sir Aillil. She met with him prior to entering the dining hall; he was standing off to the side, watching the other guests file in by pairs. The elf was a tall one, with thin straight hair that was the pale silver of the first rays of dawn. It was braided down his back, revealing his thin chin and small, pointed nose. He was a delicate-looking man, but Haven knew his swift abilities with a sword were envied on the battlefield. His eyes traveled over the guests with an almost eerie sense of knowing.

Upon seeing the princess, Ailill's eyes widened a tad from their usual half-squint, revealing both his lime-tinted irises and the surprise held in his face.

Haven approached him, a wry look on her own countenance. "What is it, Sir Ailill? Have you never seen a princess before?"

Ailill offered up his arm, his white tunic complimenting the red of Haven's gown quite nicely. "I certainly have, my lady," He began, a bemused look rising on his face. "I simply wasn't aware that there was one somewhere under that tough skin of yours."

Knowing that was about as close to a compliment as Ailill could get, Haven nodded gratefully and let herself be led forth. The duo fell in line behind Kohan and his fair lady of the evening- a daughter of some duke or another- and waited patiently for their turn. Haven broke protocol and reached forward to touch her elder brother on the shoulder.

The prince turned, and when he saw his little sister, his face lit up with pride. "You look lovely, Haven," he grinned, running the back of his finger along her cheek. A hint of mischievousness danced in his eyes when he added, "Now, if looks could get you along by themselves, you would be just fine."

"It would be my honor to interrupt the princess when she begins to speak foolishly," Ailill chimed in, amusement clearly written on his face as well.

Haven laughed along with them, trying not to let their jests feed into the nervousness that was forming around her like a cloud. It was at this time that trumpets could be heard from the interior of the hall; everyone formed back into their line, awaiting their summons. The towering oak doors swung inward, revealing a brightly lit scene before them. Rows and rows of tables had already been occupied by guests that had previously arrived. Colorful plumes and headdresses dotted the heads of many, gowns in all manner of styles mingled with the shining armor of knights and dark robes of scholars. An orchestra prepared for the procession that was to come; strings and lutes anticipating the call. The hall awaited.

    Kohan was summoned first; the lady at his hip rose to her full height, knowing it was an honor to be led into court by the prince. His visage was greeted with cheers and a unanimous round of applause. It was a given that the prince was popular amongst his people, but it still took Haven aback as to exactly how much fame he carried. Elves were not a greatly enthusiastic people, and much of their lives went on in reserved quietude. It intrigued Haven that her elder brother could solicit such a response from his subjects. She had yet to discover what exactly made him so magnetic. Kohan smiled openly and waved, exchanging greetings with those that stood closest to him. The two filed down the aisle lined with subjects and rose up a small flight of marble stairs to stand in their places at the table for royals. It stood above and perpendicular to the rest of the tables that lined the room. From his position next to the empty King's seat, Kohan winked at Haven from across the hall.

    Haven tensed, knowing that she was going to be next. She considered formulating an escape plan in case the evening fell sour. "Come now, princess," Ailill cooed, glancing down at his distressed partner. "Our great she-warrior, nervous for the Spring Revival? I'm afraid it comes every year with the melting of the frost, milady."

    Haven pursed her lips, looking up at her escort, and then to the room beyond. "It's simply another battle, correct?"

    Ailill nodded approvingly, resituating his doublet. "And you do sorely hate to lose. Don't let them steal this evening from you, Haven." He looked forward again, standing still as stone, waiting for his name to be called. Haven gripped his arm a little tighter than was normally accepted, but the elf didn't seem to mind. She sighed, thankful for his tolerance.

"And now we invite to the court, Princess of Eringoth Haven Cendra, accompanied by her escort, the esteemed Sir Ailill Algernon," The master of ceremonies called, his voice echoing throughout the entire room.

Haven refused to freeze up, and it was she who took the first step. Walking into the light was nearly blinding at first; it took her human eyes longer to adjust that it did for Ailill. She fell in step with him and held her head high.

There was a fair amount of clapping, though most it seemed almost obligatory compared to the raucous cheers that Kohan had received. By now, Haven had learned to look straight forward, staring at no one, emerald eyes twinkling. She heard her fellow knights clapping the loudest- she allowed herself to glance over and smile at them. Gideon had raised his applauding hands up, to communicate his respect. She knew that the subjects would be staring- in previous years those aloof eyes would have scalded her- but she pressed forward, wearing a faint smile. Haven knew they would be looking at her bandage, whispering about what had happened.

Haven didn't trip- and she didn't bring Ailill down with her- so when they arrived at their assigned seats, Haven considered her debut to be fairly successful. All that was left to do was await the arrival of the King, and then the feast could commence. Haven stared down at the empty silver platters before her, half trying to recall which utensil was used for what course, and consoling her rumbling stomach that food was on the way. She stood at her place with Ailill to her left and Kohan's date to her right.

The hall hushed and the orchestra softened until it was only a whisper. The master of ceremonies, a shorter elf clad in the royal red and white, stood on his podium and cleared his throat. "I now have the honor of introducing our lord King and ruler of this prosperous land of Eringoth. Having ruled these lands for nigh three and a half decades, we have seen many bright and new springs under his Highness. May the Goddess continue to bless her ruling child and guide him in her ways. Northern court, hail to your lord, King Dromo."

The room stood still as the great king entered, the clacking of his boots resonating in all corners of the hall. The great elf emerged from the wide oak doors, standing alone. His classic silk garments were complimented by a rose-colored cape and a deep maroon doublet. A sword hung at his side, unused for many years. It was a living relic in the North, known for its aid in Dromo's battles. As he strode down the aisle, the subjects he passed traced the tops of their eyelids and then held their hands out, palms upward, in an ancient gesture of deference. There was no applause, no cheers, simply revered silence. Even the Council of Elders bowed their heads as he passed them by- they may have politically disagreed on several fronts, but Dromo was still the ruler of Eringoth, and they were still his subjects.

Dromo walked up the marble stairs, his cape flowing like a waterfall in reverse motion. He stood at his ornately carved seat at the center of the royal table. The king nodded to the dignitaries to his left and right before stepping forward, arms spread outward, to address his people.

"My children," Lord Dromo began, his voice was no higher than a regular conversational tone, but it somehow managed to reach everyone in the room. "It is on this rather gloomy evening that we gather to celebrate the Goddess's great renewal of the earth." Almost as if on cue, lightning lit the long thin windows and was followed shortly by the low voice of thunder. "The rain that batters these castle walls will soon seep into the earth, bringing forth new life and a new beginning for all the land of Eringoth. The Goddess reminds us with her rains that the storm of today will summon many beautiful flowers for tomorrow. In our hearts we will carry the spirit of spring, and light these halls with our mirth as we celebrate the Revival. In the spirit of new beginnings, I have invited some honored guests to our home this evening, and I bid you all to welcome them into your hearts."

At this point in time, Dromo gestured to one of the tables closest to his own seat, where a group of men was sitting. They wore muted clothing of fairly modest means, but had beautiful fur accents that marked them as well-moneyed men. Haven hadn't noticed them before, but bit back a look of surprise when she took in exactly who they were.

It was a small party of humans, a dozen or so, and they pricked into rigid posture when attention was called to them. They seemed to be calm and well-maintained enough, not stupid or barbaric as all of her elfin teachers had described them. Haven had forgotten that her father had invited these human merchants from the periphery towns on the Peotac Mountains. Recalling now, she remembered her father saying how they hailed from a village called Trinity Heart, a fairly prosperous settlement nestled in a valley of the peaked mountains. Undoubtedly this was another one of Dromo's attempts to integrate the two worlds. And from the looks of either party, the first impressions could have been worse.

Dromo shifted back to facing the entire audience after receiving reverent bows from the human merchants. "We also have the honor of hosting the famed Eastern Battalion, known throughout the land for their skill in the arts of battle. To our cousins who hail from the seas, we are grateful that you arrived safely from your journey. I extend my kingdom's deepest sympathy at your company's loss, and I will ask the room for a moment to pray for those who did not arrive to the North this day." The hall, though silent before, became laden with the sense of deep prayer. Every soul in the room- including the humans- bowed their head out of respect for the dead.

The King looked out again over his guests, and solemnly continued to the end of his speech. "Thank you all. Without further ado, I bid all of my brothers and sisters to partake in the festivities of the evening. May the Goddess smile down on each and every one of your souls."

A quiet trailed at the end of the speech before Dromo took his seat. As he did so, the rest of the hall followed suit. The brief pause was broken upon the entrance of the multiple courses of food. From the back kitchens emerged a line of pages and squires, sporting silver platters that contained all manner of delightful foods. Everyone looked on in anticipation as the hall flooded with glinting silverware. Almost immediately the atmosphere of the room lightened, and soon chattering and exchanged greetings filled the air. Haven grinned over the table at Fintan as he placed her portion of food in front of her. He winked and moved on his way, attending to his other patrons of the evening. Haven considered checking up on her younger friend in the kitchens later if the courtly aura became too heavy. For now, though, she was content to make conversation with Ailill and enjoy the good palace food.

As the evening wore on, Haven's plate became filled with a number of valued elfin delicacies. There was a rich carrot and tomato soup and fresh-cooked wheat bread and goat cheese sprinkled on top. The featured meat was duck, deliciously dressed in a slightly sour sauce. Haven could barely contain herself; she adored any sort of poultry. She glanced over at Ailill, who was partial to his soup.

"Tut tut, sir knight," Haven pursed her lips, unceremoniously reaching over and poking Ailill's duck with her fork. "Warriors grow weak if they don't have their meat."

The elf looked over at her; she couldn't discern whether he was mildly amused or annoyed. "And princesses get their wrists slapped when they play with other people's food." He held a butter knife experimentally in his hands.

"Now Ailill," Kohan interjected from two seats down, "I wouldn't be threatening her in such a way. Before you know it, you'll be on your backside in the joust."

Ailill cracked a grin and assented, placing the knife back on the table. Kohan's belle of the evening giggled into her napkin. Her eyes creased a little at the corners when she smiled, making her look like a pixie. Haven silently wondered where Kohan found all of these beautiful maidens. His selection seemed to be even more graceful and classy than the rest of elf-kind.

Haven remembered her manners for a moment and dropped her gaze, turning it into a nod to Kohan's guest. "Milady, I do not believe we have been personally introduced. Haven Cendra."

The girl nodded back, staring at the princess with big hazel eyes. Ginger eyelashes framed her lids and cast long shadows onto her cheeks. "I am Lady Moira. I am in the North to study to become an illuminator. It truly is an honor to be here tonight," she glanced over at Kohan, who had propped up his elbow on the table to join the conversation. His light claret eyes danced; this was clearly the setting he loved most.

"I gathered that the time was nigh to add some diversity to this stale place," Kohan piped in, flashing a quick smile at Moira. Haven wasn't precisely sure of what province the lady hailed from, but she certainly did stand out. A velvet blue dress swept around her figure and her soft smoky orange curls were bunched under a small blue hat that sat atop her head.

"There seems to be plenty of that around here, from what I have gathered," Moira replied sweetly, taking a sweeping glance at Haven and then turning again to look at the prince. "And the Eastern knights seemed to have brought some color as well."

"Pray tell, my Lord," Ailill piped up, stroking his chin with a delicate hand. The Eastern knights were meant to rendezvous with their Western counterparts, were they not?"

The prince perked up at the mentioning of the West, his ears pricked in giving attention to his knight. "They were indeed," Kohan mused. He stared for a moment, looking rather perturbed at the fish on his plate before redirecting his gaze to Ailill. "In the report the Eastern cavalry gave me, it was said that the wild boar attack threw the meeting into disarray. I'd imagined that the West would have sent an envoy that would enlighten us of their situation, but thus far the connection has remained dormant."

"That is rather concerning," Haven admitted, her brow furrowing to match her brother's.

"How so, if I may be so bold," Moira asked, covering her concerned lip with a silk glove as she spoke.

"The West, being more of a glorified principality than a kingdom, is small and remote, milady," Ailill stepped in. "That kingdom hosts some of the most weathered and skilled knights the realm has ever seen. The creatures and madmen that prowl on the edge of Western land, human and non-human, are unpredictable and dangerous."

"It is unusual for them to be late to any occasion, even if the wildes of the forrest are unkind in their travels," Haven added, drawing knowledge from previous visits. It had been a while since they hailed to the North, but she could still recall their deep blue armor, rippling in a bright wave when walking in formation.

"And the storm certainly isn't doing those poor men any favors," Moira observed. Her eyes shifted over to the long windows that lined the hall. For a moment, everyone was caught up in the storm outside. Tonight was a particularly turbulent night; debris of branches and leaves swirled about in the chaos. As lightning flickered the world seemed to be a haze of disarray, only to be draped in darkness in the next moment.

Haven felt a pang of worry in her gut for the missing men. "Brother, has the king been informed of the Western absence?"

Kohan nodded slowly. "I am positive that he has discovered that fact for himself." He thought for another moment, and then stood, folding his napkin neatly on his plate. "Though I shall address it with him presently. If the men are out there- which I am sure they are- I assume that assistance will be required." He glanced apologetically at Moira and bowed low to her.

Moira waved his bow away with her hand- a gesture that solicited an exchanged look from Haven and Ailill- and smiled. "Do what you must, great prince. I am in perfectly fine company."

Kohan made a quick salute to Haven as he turned on his heel- the classic sign that he was going to inform her of everything later.

Ailill had been toying with his braid in one hand when he stated, "Perhaps there was more than simply an angry hoard of boars hindering the way of the knights."

The two women now focused their attention on him, both their faces holding questions as to why he made this conjecture. Moira was the first to speak. "What are you implying, my good sir?"

"It is not the way of the forest to be so outwardly unkind to our people. Granted, these lands are not hospitable. However, the fact that the rendezvous itself was compromised does raise some questions." Ailill replied, his thin eyes meeting Haven's.

"A sabotage?" Haven queried. To this, Ailill gave a slight nod.

Moira seemed perturbed. "Who or what could possibly succeed in such a feat?"

Ailill chuckled a tad at her confusion. "My good lady, elves are not Gods. We too can fall under a spell or be cut down by a sword. It merely takes a lot of effort to be subject to these things."

Haven paused for a moment and looked at her escort for the evening. She had never heard Ailill make such a concession about his own race; it was rare to hear any elf admit that they weren't perfect. However, he had been talking about elf-kind in general, not himself. She caught the subtle nuance and let a smile pass over her lips.

"Is something amusing you, princess?" Ailill asked. Moira picked up on Haven's grin and tilted her head.

Haven shook her head, still smiling. Sometimes she forgot how easy it was for these people to read her emotions. For her, reading elven faces was like trying to decipher a book of spells. For them, it was as easy as looking into the sky and discerning the weather. "I am merely tickled by the company I'm keeping, Sir Ailill."

The knight failed to understand her small prodding, but shrugged and continued on with the conversation. The three guests maintained a dialogue for a good amount of time, moving on from the subject of the missing Western knights. Haven noted to do some investigation in her own time.

Upon meeting Moira, Haven feared that she may have a problem with the young woman, but as the night wore on she grew to enjoy her company. Moira was eccentric for an elf; she made statements that at times made Haven feel uneasy, but unlike many others these declarations were not said with malice. They were simple and matter-of-fact, and Haven came to respect her directness. She even made a comment on the nature of Haven's ears- which were human in shape and something that had always been a sore spot for the princess. Ailill sensed that Haven was prickling at times, and redirected the conversation accordingly. The knight seemed to take a liking to Moira, which entertained Haven greatly. It was rare that Ailill had an interest in anything other than his sword work.

The evening ticked by, and Haven found that she was actually enjoying herself. The hall's volume had increased since the commencement of dinner- the mead and wine were beginning to take effect on the guests. Mirth was arising especially so from the humans' table, where the effects of liquor were more immediate. Haven silently hoped that no one made any fools of themselves tonight.

Kohan had returned to his place nigh a half an hour later, but almost as soon as he had seated himself, the master of ceremonies called out to everyone's attention. "My lords and ladies," He bellowed, waiting for all to direct their attention on him. "Now that our thirst has been quenched and our hunger sated, I am pleased to announce that it is time for the Revival Ball to commence!"

The stately aura that filled the hall almost immediately diminished. The torches and candles dimmed almost as if an invisible wind had swept through the hall. Haven, wary of what was to happen next, found herself leaning closer to Ailill.

"Shy of the flame, princess?" He asked her, patting her hand gently. Haven wondered if Gideon had told him of the embers incident near the sick bay.

Choosing to address the question in terms of the present, Haven replied, "Anything but, my friend. I'm simply not fond of the mages who make the flame."

Almost as if on cue, elegantly robed figures, draped in deep purple and green-hued capes entered the room. The room hushed until the quiet was so pronounced that one could hear the cloaks sliding along the floor. The elves stood in two straight lines; a visible pale blue light had begun to encircle them. A chill seemed to permeate throughout the hall; Haven shuddered involuntarily.

Ailill didn't try hard to hide his smirk. "These are mere parlor tricks, milady," he cooed, a thin layer of mocking glazed over his tone. "And you have your faithful knight beside you for all the protection you may require."

Haven snorted. "I don't believe that thinly veiled sarcasm is very good protection."

The mages had extended their hands out toward the individuals opposite them in line, and from each of their palms soft yellow orbs of light emerged. They were chanting softly the Ancient Tongue, and though Haven's knowledge of the language was rudimentary, she could still discern what they were saying. Words of thanks to the Goddess, requests for a bountiful spring, and asking Her to help them cast her light to the world around them. Up their hands lifted, and the soft globes rose into the air. Audible gasps were heard from the merchants, whose magical experiences must have been few, if at all.

The mages continued to chant, and as the spheres rose upward, they expanded in size until they were an eagle's wingspan in diameter. The great hall was lit with a surreal light; the orbs flickered slowly, as if they contained some sort of small and precious life. Once they ceased to rise, they remained floating long after the mages let their hands fall. The surrounding torches and candles remained dimly muted, allowing for the work of the mages to shine bright above everyone's heads.

Next, the mages spread their arms out wide, and invited all of the plant life that was scattered about the room to increase tenfold in size. Ivy plants slithered up the walls, covering all visible stone. Bouquets of flowers burst forth; daffodils, delicate snowdrops, dewberries and their fruits, crocuses and irises dotted the green canvas, blooming in seconds before everyone's eyes. Thicker vines met just beneath the ceiling and intertwined together, resembling large and ancient trees knotting up and blotting out the sky. Trickling down from the canopy came smaller globes of light that were meant to represent fireflies. They flickered faster than the greater orbs above and danced freely about the room.

Despite her fear of magic, Haven was made breathless by the miracles it could produce. She knew that its effects were fleeting and that soon this dream would come to an end, but for a moment, she allowed herself to be lost in its ephemeral beauty.

The mages ceased their chant and lowered their hands once more, filing out from the direction which they came. They were escorted out by thunderous applause and cheers. Haven allowed herself to breathe again and glanced over at the humans, who were staring in awe at the forest that had just grown around them. Tables soon began to empty and the orchestra kicked into its first waltz. The ballroom floor was quite suddenly consumed by a rainbow of dancers; dresses swirled around their owners like small cyclones as ladies were led around by their partners.

*

Haven remained rooted to her seat at the Royal table, content to pick at her meal and watch the extravaganza before her. She knew soon enough that she would have to make an entry on to the scene. The princess didn't particularly mind dancing, and always enjoyed the freedom that came with flitting about the room. Dance reminded her of sword play, in the manner in which she had to be light on her feet, always anticipating the next move of her partner. The hard part was finding individuals to dance with. For the most part, everyone but the knights shied away from a dance with the half-human, and dancing with her fellow warriors wasn't always the most comfortable situation. Haven was used to dueling and fighting with her brothers in arms, not making casual conversation and bantering with them on the dance floor.

So the princess contented herself with watching the elves and sprinkling of humans below, silently longing to one year find a partner who would make dancing truly an event. She let herself drift and listened to the music.

While looking beyond at the dancers below, Haven stopped and narrowed in on one particular elf. She was tempted to rub her eyes, thinking that her sight was deceiving her. She stopped herself before she ruined her makeup. There, amongst the blur of colors and faces, stood out one.

Haven recognized him immediately and craned her neck to get a better view. The man was on the dance floor, making long strides in wide circles with his partner. Bright hair the color of straw was tied into a small ponytail at the back of his head; the hair on the top was cropped and choppy bangs swept over his forehead. She could see his leaf-green eyes, two small earths, sparkling in the lights. He stood tall over the multitude of other guests; his smile and open laughter reached her from across the room.

Without thinking, Haven rose from her seat and swept down from the table, making her way to the ballroom half of the hall. Ailill called back to her, but Haven merely waved her escort's words aside and left him with Moira at the table. She didn't notice the elves sniffing down at her; she didn't notice how her presence parted the crowds to a noticeable degree, or that nearly everyone was staring at her arm that was in the sling. The girl stopped short of the floor itself, looking about to see where the man had gone. Haven sighted him dancing his way toward her as he talked cordially with his partner. Haven stood on her tip-toes- being half human made one short in a realm of six foot tall nymphs- and grinned widely as he swirled in her direction.

The man happened to look Haven's way; their eyes locked and the man's jaw dropped. He stumbled out of step, a foot landing on his own cape as he struggled to pull himself and his partner from dance floor. The lady looked rather perturbed and confused, and upon seeing the direction in which he was headed, she shrugged his arm off and stalked away, huffing audibly.

The elf drew near, jogging at first- he didn't seem to notice that his partner had deserted him- and slowed to a halt a few feet from the princess. His eyes were wide with disbelief; his magnetic smile had broken wide open as he crossed his arms and shook his head. The man had matured since Haven had last seen him; his features were more angular and accented, but there was still something about his long lashes and delicate lips that made him seem distinctly feminine.

"Who decided to put this scholar in a suit of armor?" Haven queried, swaying up to the man, resisting the growing urge to sweep him into a hug. She had noted the green accents to his doublet and the crest of the Eastern cavalry on his breastplate.

The man didn't restrain his laughter. "Who managed to stuff this stubborn lass into a dress? Has someone gone soft?" His eyes twinkled, putting little creases at the corners when he smiled.

Haven gestured to her bandaged arm in mock annoyance. "Does it look like I've gone soft?"

The two just stared at each other for a while, still taking in the fact that the other was there. Wordlessly they embraced, still chuckling at one another. The man cared not to jostle the princess's arm, wrapping his arms around her shoulders. Her head barely touched the bottom of his chin. Some elves had stopped and stared at this open display of affection and whispered to one another. It seemed that neither of them could hear.

"It's great to see you, Leonardo," Haven said into his shirt.

"Likewise, princess," the elf called Leonardo replied, pulling away and looking at her. "The years have been good to you. You're no longer a child. Pray tell, you're not a day over twenty three are you?"

Haven waved his remarks aside. "Stop talking down to me as if you were any older. Besides, it's never nice to ask a woman of her age. Especially a woman like me." That was another trouble of being half human- no one was exactly sure how time would weather Haven. She had been following the normal pattern of both races and hit maturity at the proper time. The next phase was questionable- whether she would cease to age, continue to weather as a human, or an odd combination of the two.

Leonardo snorted and took Haven under his arm. "A woman like you comes around once in a lifetime. I need to treasure you for all the years to come. How long has it been since we last saw one another? Come, come. Let us move to a more private setting. It feels as though we're being watched," he murmured, underscoring the number of looks the pair was getting.

The two left the dance floor and the gaze of all the other guests and entered a small side-room. The ceiling was lower but made of glass, as were the other tree walls. The rain had lightened a tad and sprinkled softly above their heads. Candles flickered gently on stands. Tables and plush couches and lounge chairs were situated in cozy circles. Smaller groups of people were gathered around, talking quietly amongst themselves. No one heeded the addition of two more to the peaceful place. Haven and Leonardo picked two chairs next to one another.

Haven immediately removed her shoes and sighed with relief. "Any longer out there and I would have torn my corset off too," she said to her friend, letting herself collapse into the soft material of the chair.

"At least you have some sense of propriety," Leonardo teased, leaning into his own chair. "But I must give credit where it's due. Four years ago I wouldn't have imagined you ever properly wearing a dress."

"And four years ago I never fathomed that my dear Leonardo would become a knight!" Haven exclaimed, returning to her earlier observation. "I thought your love was for books, not the sword. You studied so long at university."

Leonardo shrugged, looking up at the ceiling, then down at her again. "I couldn't allow you to beat me as poorly as you did all those years ago."

"You have a complex now? That a girl defeated you in sword play?"

"Hardly a complex. I just hate to lose." Leonardo replied, sticking his chin out resolutely.

"That makes two of us then," Haven shot back with a smirk. "But come, Leonardo. Why alter your course?" She remembered when his hair had been long and his form had been less imposing. He still retained the ear piercings and cuffs that recognized him as a learned man, but he had become rougher around the edges. While his figure had become more full, there still seemed to be something absent about the man.

Leonardo snapped his fingers, having just come up with an idea. "What say you, to a duel one day soon when your arm is mended?"

Haven sat for a moment, thinking. He wasn't addressing her queries, which was a classic indicator that he had no intention of leading the conversation in that direction. It made her wonder, but she acquiesced to his silent request and pushed on. "I think I would be able to handle you just fine. I'm not intimidated by you simply because you have a sword at your hip."

The elf shook his head, grinning, and leaned forward. He rested his elbows on his knees and folded his hands. "Nothing intimidates you, does it?"

"That's not true at all. Quite a few things do. I simply have to get over it and keep moving forward. I'm just not scared of you, Leonardo." She pushed his shoulder.

He chuckled. "You're good not to be. I'm still the same man that I was four years ago, simply without the spectacles."

Haven's mouth dropped open- she had forgotten that aspect about her friend. "That's what it was! I knew there was something different about you."

"And you have only managed to become more beautiful, my lady," Leonardo stated, taking her hand. A sly smile had spread across his face. "The girl I used to know has become a woman."

"Calling me beautiful is like telling a pixie that it can't fly," Haven retorted, rolling her eyes. Blush had begun to prickle on her face in spite of herself. "Save it for your women back East."

Leonardo grinned, pleased that he had accomplished in making her uncomfortable. "Losing the spectacles was the first step to earning access to more courtly pleasures," he started, eyes sparking.

"Now I understand why you wanted to become a knight," Haven teased, eyeing her friend. Leonardo was a notorious flirt with all of the women at court; there was a certain charm about him, a charm that carried over through his transformation. Luckily for Haven, she seemed to be immune to these overt displays of flattery.

"Knighthood certainly has its advantages," Leonardo agreed, adjusting his cape. "but that isn't to say that I don't miss my studies."

Haven thought back to when they first met. "Did you not come to the North to investigate the royal history of Eringoth for some thesis of yours?"

"I'm surprised you remember," Leonardo commended her, eyes tinted with nostalgia. "It was for my final assessment as an understudy, to investigate the bloodline of the Cendra family through the generations."

"Which is how you came across my interesting persona," Haven concluded. "That was an amusing day." She could recall it clearly. "As a young, frustrated nineteen year old, it was certainly an odd request to be sought out by a student from Eastern university."

Leonardo chuckled. "You didn't want anything to do with me."

"I didn't want anything to do with anyone at that point," the princess countered, recalling her more confused days. "I didn't like being around elves."

Leonardo guffawed; they both knew how her dislike couldn't be avoided. "I bet you were surprised when I didn't question you about any possible extreme emotional tendencies or if you were suicidal or anything of the sort."

Haven nodded vigorously. "It was quite refreshing to hear from a man who didn't see me as an accident or an experiment. And it was nice to talk about my family for once, with someone who understood and appreciated our situation."

"Indeed. I loved hearing about your mother. She was certainly a large point in my thesis." Leonardo watched Haven upon the mentioning of May Cendra.

Only a few people addressed the existence of the now infamous May, the woman to most who had soiled the pure Cendra name. She was a very sensitive topic for Haven, because she hated when disparaging remarks began to cloud the pure memory she struggled to retain of her mother. She glanced at Leonardo, telling him with her eyes that he was fortunate to be one of the few with whom she could address this topic.

"What did you say about her?" Haven asked, curious. She had never in her letters thought to mention the end result of the report that Leonardo had composed.

"Only positive things, if that's what you are wondering," Leonardo replied, assuring her with his hand on hers that he valued her mother as she did.

Haven managed a laugh. "That must have damaged the veracity of your final assessment, then."

The knight shook his head. "My professor rather enjoyed the progressive viewpoint that I took in the study," he said in a matter-of-fact manner. "The thinkers out in the East aren't as stuffy as they're made out to be, Haven. We believe that change and progression is a part of nature. The fact that not more of our people have picked up on this pattern yet is a shame to behold."

"I agree. And I fear that the North is the stuffiest of all the Quartet Kingdoms," Haven sighed, looking out the windows before them and into the rainy evening. "My father really is trying to effect legislation that will come to accept my people. Despite the fact that he is king, he has met an enormous amount of resistance from the Council."

Leonardo rolled his eyes at the mentioning of the Elders. "All those coots are good for is being stubborn. And perhaps maintaining our history. They're sticking their noses too far into the law."

Haven nodded, thinking back on all of the times when her father would return from a meeting, his patience worn thin. "And Kohan has to play the mediator, ensuring that personal goals and vendettas on either side don't impede operations of the kingdom. It's helped him to become a stronger leader."

Her friend grimaced at the mentioning of the prince. "Is he still peeved about my last visit to the North?"

Haven laughed outright, which turned a few heads in their direction. "I had forgotten. He hasn't mentioned it to me in quite some time; I hope for your sake he's forgotten it as well."

The last time that Leonardo had come to the Northern Kingdom, Haven had convinced him to steal away a woman from Kohan, because she wasn't good for the prince and he was beginning to neglect his duties to the kingdom on her account. Haven had failed to mention the fact that she also envied the woman for all the attention she was getting from Kohan. So she employed Leonardo to do what he did best; the result was a rather put off prince and mission accomplished.

"It's not the greatest position to be in, being on the prince's bad side," Leonardo stated. "You're a lucky lass that I do all of the things I do for you."

Haven mused for a moment, looking into the eyes of her friend. "And I believe I have just found another use for you, dear Leonardo." She stood then, not waiting for a reply, and began to replace her shoes on her feet. Seeing as this was almost impossible, Leonardo bent down to her feet and laced the shoes back on for her.

"What is that mind of yours scheming now, little princess?" he asked, looking up at her from the ground. Haven held her arm out to him as he stood; he took it accordingly. "I do believe this is supposed to be the other way around," he chuckled, amused at Haven's attempt at masculinity.

"You have longer eyelashes than I do, so it's only fair that I lead you back into the ballroom for a dance." Haven's eyes glinted deviously as she tried to tug Leonardo back into the ballroom.

"You only have to ask, Haven," the knight said, gently switching places so that her arm rested on the inside of his. Haven looked up into Leonardo's open face and smiled. The man exhaled. "I suppose that's almost as good as saying 'please'".

So the two friends re-entered the throng of guests, elves and humans alike. The air of the place had relaxed considerably. A few humans, emboldened by the beverages, had stepped up to elves to make conversation and overall, things seemed to be going well. To be sure, the elves seemed hesitant as to how to carry out a conversation with such an emotional and vibrant people. But they seemed intrigued for the most part, listening to stories about the small trading outposts that the merchants hailed from and hearing about life on the other side of the Petoac Mountains.

Haven peered around for her father and brother as she and Leonardo took to the dance floor, but neither of them could be sighted. She pursed her lips in thought as they prepared to dance. The music halted as dancers bustled about, searching for new partners or refreshments. The lights danced all around the guests, casting odd shadows on the vines that covered the walls. It gave the impression of specters and intangible creatures joining in on the festivities.

The music started up again. It was odd as first, trying to get around Haven's cast, but eventually they fell into a comfortable rhythm. After getting accustomed to the pattern, Haven recognized the song that they were dancing to. The Dance of Daffodils.

A wide grin broke across Leonardo's face as he began to lead Haven around the floor. "How fortunate, the Goddess has looked down upon us this fine evening," he declared, looking up to the heavens as if searching for a form to give thanks to.

"This dance isn't just for lovers," Haven grumbled, suddenly wary of any eyes that may have been following her around the room.

"Oh, but it is," he declared, voice rising to theatrical tones. "The blossoming of the fair daffodil in the spring is akin to the blossoming of sweet love, small and pure."

"I don't know much about that," retorted Haven, brushing aside Leonardo's antics. "But I can tell you that I would dance this dance with you as a sign of the renewal of our friendship after a winter of distance apart." She dodged away from the topic of romance; the last thing she needed to worry about was her love life. Well, she rarely had to- few inhabitants of the Quartet Kingdoms had taken an interest in Dromo's only daughter. Not that she particularly minded- Haven never had time to entertain the thought of having a lover.

Leonardo chuckled. "Have it your way. This is your dance, after all. I'm honored that you have chosen me as your partner."

"You know it was completely on accident," Haven reminded him.

"I think it was simply meant to be," he countered, leading her under his arm for a twirl. "And how perfect, to be serendipitously reunited like this."

Haven came in close to him again, feeling his firm hand on her waist, bringing them closer together. It was nice to be held, she realized. "It truly is good to see you again, old friend," she smiled.

As it was accustomed in this particular dance, the music slowed when it reached the middle of the piece. Couples all around halted their pace, circling each other gently. With the faltering of the music came the dimming of the large yellow globes in the ceiling, which draped the room in a comforting dim.

Haven felt the activity of the day and of the evening begin to weigh down on her; the joust and the surgery, her verbal battle with Unus, the anxiety that accompanied the Revival, all began to prey on her physical state. It was as if a blanket of exhaustion had just laid itself over her entire being.

She looked up at Leonardo, then at the people that surrounded them, and then finally let herself lay her head on the knight's chest. The girl wasn't sure if she felt a sharp intake of breath from her friend, or if her tired mind was playing tricks on her. Almost in response, Leonardo wrapped his arm around her shoulders and pulled her in close. She loved the sense of comfort that always accompanied his presence; it felt as if a fortress had been built around her. For once, she didn't have to worry about anything but the safety she felt in her friend's arms.

"I've missed you," she mumbled into his shirt for the second time that evening. The princess felt her walls crumbling for the first time in a long while, and let herself collapse into her friend.

Leonardo squeezed her good shoulder and leaned over to whisper in her good ear. "I've missed you too, little lady. This austere Northern landscape is just a little brighter with you here."

Haven sighed, feeling the warmth of his chest and recalling his familiar scent; of fresh sea air and sharp dune grass. It was as if he had just walked off of a merchant ship. She let the scent carry her away, far to the East, where the white-columned structures clustered around sparkling hot springs and the ocean hushed contentedly in the background. The sky was a bright cerulean blue and towering cotton-ball clouds rolled overhead.

"Promise you'll take me with you one day," Haven found herself saying. "I want to see the white towers again." She had only been there once, as a small infant, while on a trip with her brother. Everything was in a haze.

Leonardo seemed amused at Haven's sudden shift in thought. "If you let me beat you in that duel you promised, I might be able to arrange something."

Haven opened her eyes to find herself aligned with Sir Gideon and another woman. The man was grinning openly at her and the unknown Eastern knight, eyes twinkling deviously. Haven rolled her eyes and ignored the Captain of the Guard as he floated past. He was mouthing words to her, but she opted to continue her conversation. "Speaking of duels, where were you this afternoon? I'm positive you heard of my little bout."

The knight laughed. "Why else would I have refrained from asking of your sling? I wanted you to be the one to address it first."

"How kind of you," Haven muttered, half sarcastic. She had caught him looking down at her arm with mild concern a few times previously in the evening.

"I was actually doing some intelligence research with a couple of the locals at the time of your battle with Sir Mordred, the Mallard Knight." He declared rather enigmatically. "He's a fiery fellow, too. We never really take him seriously anyway."

It dawned on her after a time about what exactly Leonardo meant. She looked up at him, curious. "Were these locals...rather furry and small?"

Leonardo grinned; she felt his chuckle through the hand that had come to rest on his chest. "Most of them were, yes. Others were larger and some had wings, too."

It wasn't uncommon for elves to be born with a power additional to their extra-long life, natural beauty, calm disposition and deft athleticism. For some, this meant that they could heal with their magic, control the elements like water or wind, read minds, and the like. Leonardo was gifted with a rather unique skill; he had the power of talking to all manner of creatures. Upon first telling the girl, he batted his eyes and said he had a gifted tongue. She had made him demonstrate his power for her by conversing with a muskrat on how to build a lodge; it was truly a remarkable experience.

"What sort of intelligence were you looking for?" the princess asked, brow furrowed.

Leonardo sighed, and his voice grew hard. "We lost a lot of good knights out there on the road to this kingdom." Haven looked into his face; it had become uncharacteristically stony. He peered down at her, his usually light eyes filled with remorse. She was starting to realize how knighthood may have changed him after all. "That boar attack was unsolicited. I was asking local boar tribes and other traveling animals what had happened."

"What did they say?" Haven asked, intrigued. It seemed that Ailill wasn't the only one with his suspicions on the attack.

Leonardo bit his lip, formulating his thoughts. Evidently the results were confusing- that or he was translating what he had heard into the normal tongue. "I was told that a tribe south of here was driven off course by a disturbing, unnatural force. The leader was driven mad; something had convinced him that my band of knights had killed his family."

Haven stuck out her lip, more confused than ever. "How does that even happen? You didn't kill any boars, did you?"

Leonardo shook his head. "Nothing of the sort. We didn't see any in the entirety of our journey, until they were right on top of us." He involuntarily shuddered, remembering something that he didn't elect to mention. "But what concerns me even more is that the Western knights were not at the designated meeting point."

This was news to Haven. The girl waited for Leonardo to continue; there was plainly more to his tale by the look on his face.

"This may sound odd," He said, looking down at Haven, eyes slimmed in thought. "But I thought I heard a voice inside my head. It was before the animals came cracking down. And then I could have sworn I saw a man in the woods. Dressed in black from head to toe in robes that I've never seen before. He was staring at me; I could have sworn that his eyes were red." He faltered, shaking his head, knowing how crazy it sounded. Haven patted his chest, assuring that she both believed him and wanted him to continue. "It was far away though, so I could be wrong. But I heard a voice."

Haven was silent for a moment, picturing the man in her own head. He stood here, on a ledge of rock that was jutting out of the side of the mountain. Shadows were his friend; most of his being was wreathed in the colors of the forest, undetectable and unseen. But the look Haven had seen in Leonardo's face painted the red eyes in her vision. They glowed, like hot embers on a dying flame. She inhaled deeply, allowing the sight to trickle from her view. "What was the voice saying, Leonardo?" Haven asked, turning back to him. The dance around them had begun to speed up again; couples took to swirling about the room once more. Haven and Leonardo remained as they were before, transfixed on their conversation.

Leonardo closed his eyes, trying to concentrate in the din of the ballroom. "I recognized the words as being from the ancient tongue," he started, thinking hard. "But it was different. The words were broken and some of them I couldn't even recognize. I'd never heard the likes of it before. It sounded like whoever it was…was casting a spell."

Haven was about to ask for an extrapolation, but her thoughts were interrupted by a shriek that cut through the atmosphere as a knife cuts through cloth. Quickly followed by that scream was a burst of bright yellow light, then the sound of bodies crumpling to the floor. Music dwindled and faltered to a stop, strings sliding uncomfortably across instruments. The two friends were startled from their embrace and like everyone else on the floor, looked to the direction from which the scream came.

"What was that?" Haven's bewildered eyes traced about the room, searching for clues.

Leonardo gestured to a growing crowd a little ways from them. The shrieks had turned to sobs and there was shouting from several men. Haven saw her brother rush into the fray. One hand was on the hilt of his sword. "Wait here," Leonardo said as he began to make his way toward the collection of people.

"No way," Haven retorted, gathering her skirts and falling in stride with him. Leonardo didn't fight her, and instead offered his hand while he began to elbow his way through the onlookers. Haven clasped his hand and filed in after him, letting the larger man forge a path in the crowd.

"Prayers to the sweet Goddess," someone mumbled as Haven walked by.

"Now somebody tell me. What has happened here?" The girl heard her elder brother ask, his voice crisp and authoritative. "Sir Gideon, hail for a Healer at once."

In moments, the Captain was seen shouldering through the guests with blood on his open palms. Gideon shot Haven a heavy glance as he brushed by. Leonardo had finally made his way to the front; Haven forged a spot beside him. She clapped a gloved hand to her mouth at the scene before her.

A she-elf wearing a sleeveless green ball gown was collapsed on the floor, surrounded by three other elves. She was crying, her extravagant makeup made black streaks on her pale cheeks. Her head was in the chest of a knight who had been murmuring reassuringly to her, a hand on her delicate shoulder.

On the ground near the woman lay a human- one of the merchant party. He was sprawled on his back as if he had been forced backward with great power. The side of his head looked as if it had been bludgeoned; blood trickled from the side of his face and pooled in a gleaming mess on the stony floor. Hair at the side of his head was matted with blood and one eye had sealed up from swelling. His left hand was greatly bloodied as well, the fingertips worn raw by some sort of friction or heat.

Kohan was knelt over the human, assessing the damage. He was barking orders to the knights on call and constantly checking the pulse of the man at his feet.

Haven stared in horror, sending several prayers to the Goddess, begging for the man's life to be spared. She feared what it would mean for future cooperation between the two races, should this man die.

This thought was also cut short by another shout, this one more deep and menacing. Bursting forth from the crowd came another merchant, dagger raised high above his head. His eyes were flickering with rage, all of his force bent on reaching his comrade. His gaze fixated on Kohan- who was still knelt over the victim's body- and the man shrieked again, tilting into the circle straight for the prince.

Leonardo instinctively lunged forward. Haven felt the palms of her gloves beginning to smoke.

Five

AAREN

THERE WAS SCREAMING. Bodies running, falling, trampling. The hot scent of sulfur and magic was married to the poignant odor of fresh blood. Red was everywhere, spattered on doors and windows, beneath the feet of unbridled terror.

Then, the overwhelming sense of helplessness. The world seemed to fall into a dim shade, noises muffled and vision blurred. Nothing can be done; all is lost. The hole deep inside begins to grow, to overtake, to conquer. Closing hands into tight fists- there is nothing more terrible than a helpless ruler. He wished for death, but death did not notice, and it passed him by. Not unscathed, but soul intact. Living with nothing to live for.

So this is what Chaos feels like.

A soft hand gently touched the forehead of the unconscious man. He recoiled from the touch instantly; the hand left his range of senses as a light would leave the room. Through his half-awake state, Aaren wondered if he had been touched by the Goddess. If she was telling him to get up. The fight was not yet over.

Aaren sensed that he was no longer in the cave in which he fell asleep; the air surrounding him was comfortably warm and dry. In the far edge of his senses, he heard a fire crackling in a hearth, and the scent of herbs boiling wafted over to him. The hard ground under his back was replaced with a soft down comforter and pillow.

The only odd contrast about all of these feelings was that the elf felt cool droplets forming on his face. They dripped onto his skin, one by one, and Aaren couldn't help but flinch at their cold sting. An almost noiseless sniff accompanied these drops, and he discerned the coolness to be tears.

Aaren opened his eyes. Inhabiting most of his vision was a young woman, light hazel eyes shimmering with salty tears and a mass of brunette curls spilling forth from a dark hood. She was pale, presumably from the cold and the storm of the outdoors, but there was a strength in her eyes that kindled a fire in Aaren's own cold heart. The clear streaks continued to run down her face, a continuous flow. She girl's mouth was a firm small line, but her chin quivered ever so slightly when a tear dripped from her face.

When she realized that the man was waking, she girl inhaled quickly, eyes brimming over with fresh tears. "I am so sorry," she breathed, her voice barely above a whisper. "If there was anything in the world I could do. Anything that could take back what I've done…" She trailed off, eyes closing. It seemed to be her own discipline that kept her from breaking down.

Without thinking, Aaren reached up with a weak hand, rubbing the tears away from the girl's cheek with his thumb. She immobilized at his touch, watching him with wide, grieving eyes. He didn't know what this girl was talking about, why she was so sad, but he couldn't bear to see her so upset. "You haven't done anything wrong," Aaren murmured through his drowsiness. "Please don't cry."

It seemed as if this woman was draining Aaren of all grief and taking it upon herself. With every moment that his fingers lingered on her skin, the drier he began to feel, as if she was absorbing his tears and expelling them for him. She woman had placed her hand over his, burying her face in his palm. The soft wet eyelashes tickled his bruised skin.

"It's my fault, all my fault," the girl persisted weakly, giving in to Aaren's touch. The hood had fallen back from her head, revealing chestnut-colored hair in a mangle of braids and flowers. Human ears, rounded off, peeked out from her brown locks.

Aaren shook his head weakly. "If it's anyone's fault, it is my own," he said, looking into her face. The elf wasn't exactly sure what he was blaming himself for. Anything to keep this woman from crying any longer. It hadn't yet registered for him what a human was doing on the Eastern side of the Petoac Mountains.

The girl's pink lips parted as if she wanted to say something more, but they closed again, unsure of how to continue. Her eyes glimmered in the firelight of the nearby hearth; an otherworldly glow flickered in her pupils. She looked away from him for a moment, and then turned back, contemplating. Wordlessly, she inclined her head over the wounded Aaren, momentarily hovering over his face before pressing her lips to his.

Aaren jolted fully awake at her close proximity, the alien feeling of lips on his own sounding an alarm throughout his entire being. He tensed up and pulled away, eyeing the woman with a guarded gaze. She stared at him, her visage draped in sadness. "I'm sorry," she whispered, dropping her gaze. "I want to make things better."

Utterly baffled and confused, it took several moments for Aaren to filter what had just happened. He stared back at the girl, her figure delicate and alone. He felt himself being filled with regret for making her look at him in such a way. With his hand he again beckoned her closer, and welcomed her kiss for a second time. Reason was willing him to pull away again, but there was something magnetic about her that brought the elf to collapse into her kiss instead. Unfamiliar warmth caressed his lips, so gentle and faint that he felt himself reciprocating the fragility for fear of breaking the connection forged with this unnamed woman.

A new voice broke the spell.

"Millie. What in the world are you doing to our guest?" A man's crisp tone forced Aaren and the woman apart. He savored the lingering warmth on his lips.

Aaren pulled back, for the first time getting a sense of the space that he was occupying. He was inside a one-room cottage no larger than several horse stalls. All manner of living materials were scattered about the place- hand-woven quilts, gardening implements, cooking utensils, extra bedding and freshly washed clothes. Dried herbs hung suspended from the exposed rafters above, their delicate scents intermingling and floating downward. As he had guessed, off to the side there was a small flickering fire with a black pot situated over the flame. For some reason, no matter how Aaren tried, he could not focus on any one particular object. From his peripherals, the setting seemed perfectly clear. He would then attempt to look directly at something and all would fall into a fuzzy glow. The elf shook his head, thinking his frail condition was to blame.

    The only object that was in clear focus was the owner of the disruptive voice. Aaren looked up; a man stood in the open doorway, the outside night quiet but still heavy with dampness from the recent storm. His presence filled the room, almost to the point where everything was dwarfed by him. The man was draped in a long black cloak that swept about his toes; the bottom and the edges of the sleeves were laden with silver knots and encryptions with which Aaren was unfamiliar. Pitch black hair, locks void of all color and sprinkled with braids framed a weathered face. The man's face held strong features, chiseled and worn from years of strife. Not an ounce of extra fat lay on the man's skin, and underneath the cloak Aaren could discern dense muscle mass.

    What fascinated Aaren was the fact that the man seemed to be neither elf nor human; the quiet aura that surrounded him wrapped his identity in secrecy. His ears were covered by his black locks; Aaren couldn't tell whether they were pointed or rounded. There was something supernatural about the man that put the elf on alert.

    But the one thing that both perturbed and intrigued Aaren was a particular quality about the man's face.

    He had red eyes.

    The irises burned dimly, resembling molten lava churning passively at the mouth of a volcano. They watched Aaren with intelligence, but underneath that layer of sophistication Aaren could see a world of torment and demonic thought.

    Aaren lay silent, taking in the man before him and thinking on every option that he had. The mysterious man had blocked the door, the only obvious escape other than a few small glass windows. He didn't seem to be openly threatening, but Aaren knew that he was in the presence of a killer. Aaren eyed the man and remained on his cot, waiting for him to make the next move. There was a reasoning behind all of this. Aaren decided to let everything play out.

The girl who responded to the name Millie jolted upright and stood, facing the man. Her lip trembled but her eyes were no longer laden with tears.

"I didn't order you to fraternize with our guest, Millie." The man said, taking a step forward and closing the door behind him. When he looked at her, there was an uncharacteristic tenderness, but his voice held a sharp severity that contradicted his look. "Address his wounds, and then be gone. Is it that hard to understand?"

Millie bowed low. "I was trying to make amends." Her voice sounded distant; it echoed as if she was talking from the other end of a long hallway.

"Get out of my sight." The man's voice was bitter. He gestured to the door and stepped aside to let her pass.

Millie didn't look at Aaren as she rose to leave. She opened the door but stopped just before stepping out into the forest. Reaching out, she touched the collar of his sleeve in the delicate manner that she carried. The man refrained from meeting her eyes, as if looking at her might just be the last thing he could ever do. Resigned, Millie walked out into the woods, tossing the cloak over her head. "I'll be waiting on the other side," she murmured as she left, voice echoing in the small room.

Aaren watched Millie leave, completely perplexed. He could not discern the relationship she held with the mysterious man with the red eyes, nor could he reckon where she was headed. Aaren watched as she went into the darkness, and became even more confused upon her sudden vanishing. Blinking twice, he looked hard into the darkness. Mist was crawling forth from the mouth of the words, but Millie hadn't even made it that far. She merely faded from existence- first the edges of her physique became blurred. Then they frayed, unraveling like a poorly knitted scarf, until all of the strands disappeared, carried away in an invisible wind.

Before Aaren could ask any questions, the man in black slammed the door shut and bolted the lock. When his hand left the knob, a spark of blue magic traced between his figure and the metal. He strode over and stood at the foot of Aaren's cot, resting a foot on the wooden frame. He remained motionless, gazing at Aaren with smoldering eyes.

"What were you doing in the middle of the Forrest?" He asked cooly, as if the girl named Millie hadn't even been present moments before.

"How did I get here?" Aaren countered, determined not to relay any information until he had his questions answered. He was half afraid to recount what exactly had brought him into the middle of the dark woods.

A smirk spread across the man's face. "I brought you here. You were alone, dying in a dark cave."

"Why save me?" Aaren fired next, eyeing the man guardedly.

"Frankly, I would have left you there, but you have a very curious trinket on your person that I've taken quite an interest in," the man stated, leaning in so he could better study the elf.

Aaren stopped for a moment, perplexed. "I have nothing of value. All I own has been lost." Saying the phrase aloud was like getting kicked in the chest.

The mysterious man shook his head, grin growing even wider. He motioned to Aaren's neck. "The plates on your collar. They won't come off, will they?"

Instinctively, Aaren's hand fluttered to his throat, where he could feel the cool metal snug against his skin. He inhaled and closed his eyes, saying nothing. Swallowing was difficult.

"The necklace is cursed, Prince Aaren." The man murmured. Aaren looked up, startled at the sound of his own name.

"Yes, I know who you are, second son of King Ronan and Queen Talulla. Do you know who gave you that cursed trinket?"

Aaren felt his heartbeat begin to quicken. He shook his head.

"You're lying." The man accused flatly.

The prince shut his eyes, trying to force out the memories that were attempting to break down his walls. The pain was so fresh and so real. He would be reliving it again soon enough.

"Answer me, your highness," The man ordered, his voice tinged with sarcasm. "Or I'll cut open all of the wounds that my dear Millie had painstakingly healed for you." Threatening crept into his voice; Aaren looked up and found the man to be rising to his full height.

Aaren knew he was in no position to bargain. He closed his eyes shut and then opened them again, hoping to cloud away the pain in his heart. "It was Lord Inness. He did this to me," Aaren whispered, looking away, unconsciously feeling the necklace that hugged his throat.

It seemed as though the man had gotten the answer he was searching for; he pulled away and resumed his stance at the foot of the cot. Aaren's words were some sort of confirmation to the man of information unknown to the prince. The look on the man's face was a medley of satisfaction and discontent at the same time.

"What's it to you who gave me this cursed object?" Aaren asked, gulping down his emotions and focusing on the man in front of him. He needed answers, now. For the first time he completely took in the figure before him, who clearly had as much emotional tumult as he did. "Who are you?"

The man tilted his head back, still peering down at Aaren but allowing the glow of the firelight to compliment his own burning eyes. "Some call me Aki." As a smirk twisted across his face, the lights in room seemed to darken, as if muted by the power that emanated from the enigmatic figure at the mentioning of his own name.

"What is your purpose here? Why did you save me?" Aaren persisted, struggling into a sitting position so that he could see his savior and interrogator more clearly.

The man called Aki chuckled darkly and shook his head. "Those queries, little prince, are better left unanswered. But I can tell you about the trinket you wear." He began to stride about the room, pacing back and forth, eyes always on Aaren. "Lord Inness placed a very damning spell on you indeed; he meant for you so suffer. You won't realize it right away, but with time the metal plates will begin to converge, cutting your breath short and sapping your strength. These plates will slowly suffocate you until they steal the last breath away from your lungs, and you will die."

Aaren touched the cold killers at his neck once more and felt his heart drop. Inness truly did want him dead after all. He couldn't bring himself to speak.

"With my assistance, however, I may be able to rid you of your curse." Aki continued. He stopped pacing and faced Aaren squarely. "It will require doing something that you may outright protest, but there is no other way. You can accept your fate and die as a coward, or you can fight for your life, and attempt to alter the hand that the Goddess has given you."

Aaren looked down into his lap, at the hands that rested there, limp. He was so weak. They reflected the rest of his body-battered and scraped and worn, but still operational. He still had strength yet. Was there something he could do? Or was it all futile? His people were lost; he had no one to preside over and therefore had lost his purpose.

"I know what you're thinking," Aki started, moving closer to Aaren once more. "I can feel it in the emotions that are rolling off of your pathetic body. Do you not want to avenge those who were lost? Or are you going to curl up and die, leaving their memories to the mountain on which they were slain? What kind of prince are you?" His accusing eyes pierced Aaren's own cerulean ones. A flicker of anger passed through Aaren's face; he bit his lip to keep from saying anything threatening to the omniscient man.

Aaren didn't even question how Aki had known the events of the preceding day. The man was very well-informed. It was something that Aaren simply had to accept- for he spoke the truth. Was Aaren really going to allow himself to fall into the pit of his own despair? There was a duty to his people that he still held, even in light of the recent tragedy: justice had to be served.

Aki waited patiently for Aaren to muddle through his thoughts; he sensed there was a resolution of sorts making its way to the surface. When Aaren looked up again, there was a new strength simmering underneath the ocean blue of his eyes. "What do I have to do?" He asked firmly.

"You must face the sorcerer who bestowed upon you that cursed trinket," Aki declared. Another smirk sprouted on his face. "And you must take back what is rightfully yours."

Aaren felt the blood drain from his cheeks, but his expression remained steadfast. The man in black sneered at Aaren's change in pallor.

"But you cannot do it alone," Aki continued, rising again to pace around the room, arriving at a window. He stared out into the early morning gloom. The mist curled up from the high woodland grasses and shrubs, twisting and bending around the arms of the ancient trees. Aki eyed the light yellow disc, wrapped in grey clouds that had begun to rise out of the trees. "You must ride to the North, as fast as your soul can carry you, and get help. They've been amassing warriors there for some time now."

"Why are you helping me?" Aaren asked, still quite mystified as to the motives behind this man. "I have no knowledge of who you are."

Aki refrained from turning from the window, but his voice carried an undeniable bitterness. "And it is better that you have no knowledge of who I am. I only ask one favor of you." It took Aaren a moment to realize, but Aki's figure had begun to fray as Millie had several minutes before. The man looked at Aaren with his smoldering eyes, which were still sharp and crisp. "When you do meet Lord Inness again, please inform him that his old friend Aki sends his regards."

Aaren watched, speechless, as Aki's form began to tear away at the edges. His cloak ripped and frayed, more violently so that Millie's form had. Everything about the man had begun to dematerialize. Aaren looked above his head- the thatched ceiling had begun to leak clear rainwater- it spattered on his clothes and made the fire hiss. The prince felt his own vision blurring; the world began to swirl into darkness. The cottage around him spun into a vortex, everything inside it being twisted into unnatural jagged shapes. The world had gone silent when Aaren lost consciousness. The last thing he could remember was those two burning red eyes, staring at him.

Six
LEONARDO

IT WAS A LONG WALK from the Northern Palace to the fringe of the Royal Forrest. Leonardo didn't particularly mind. It had been so long since he'd made the trek to the periphery of civilization that Haven had to lead him there. He smiled at the back of her figure, draped in a simple tunic and black britches, as she led him from the entrance hall and out the two grand front doors of the castle.

The knight was met with the gleaming rays of the midmorning sun, a welcoming presence after a long night of rain and wind. The many flights of white stairs that led to the mouth of the castle shimmered. Puddles of rainwater reflected the sun's light. Down below the Northern City lay spread out beneath him, waiting to be explored. Surrounded by a high white wall, the town below was just waking up to start another long work day.

Before him at the bottom of the stairs lay a long isle, an expanse of green grass and willow trees that stood on either side like permanent sentries. Leonardo was aware that he stood at the spot where great kings of the past and present made their speeches to the Northern people, who would gather in the green below and listen. In his mind the space below him filled with people, every last one was staring right at him. To his left and right, Northern banners flapped in a slight breeze. Placing his fists on his hips and puffing out his chest, he imagined what it would be like to project to all of these people. What it would be like to be heard.

Haven stopped and turned, beckoning for her friend to catch up with her. He broke his reverie when their eyes met. "Why the long pause, Leonardo? Don't you want me to share my secret with you?"

Haven had hinted that morning at breakfast that there was a place in the Royal Forrest that Leonardo would take quite an interest in. A part of his mind couldn't help but wonder why she wanted to draw him so far from society. He tried to tell himself that it wasn't because she wanted to be alone with him. The thought, however, refused to leave his mind.

Leonardo grinned down at the princess, who was evidently excited for the journey ahead. "Of course I do, lass," he started, moving to catch up with her. "It has been a while since I've taken in the view of this magnificent place. My memory serves the reality quite poorly." The people crowding around the green melted away as he fell in step with the princess.

Haven led Leonardo down the center of the green, talking away as they went. She motioned to the great willow trees and how their roots had been growing in this land for centuries. Leonardo looked into the vines and saw small houses carved into the roots, windows formed from knots in the trunks and doors hidden carefully away from sight. If a human had walked down this aisle of trees, they would not have known that they were surrounded by elfin dwellings.

"The Elders and powerful mages live here, if my memory serves me correctly," Leonardo conjectured, eyeing a nearby abode as they passed.

Haven nodded, heaving a breath. "It's a shame that the Council has to take up such a nice place, though I don't mind the mages and sorcerers that make a home here. They deserve to live in such honorable dwellings."

"I thought you despised magic," Leonardo asserted, looking at the girl beside him. She avoided his gaze by continuing to observe the trees around them.

"Magic is a mysterious thing. I may not understand it but that doesn't mean that I despise it," she dodged around the allegation, rubbing her hands together. "Besides. The mages that live here are an asset to the North, in all manner of wisdom, history and healing."

With that, Haven decided she was finished speaking of magic, and resolved to skip down the green lane. Young spring flowers bowed to the princess as her feet glided over them; bugs and pollen sprung up from the ground as she went, leaving a cloud of nature in her wake. She turned and beckoned again to Leonardo, who was obliged to run after her because she refused to let him catch up.

Out of breath, the two finally stopped at a set of gates of iron. Metal vines twisted up toward the sky in a swirling of organized chaos. The gates stretched upward of fifteen feet and when closed, could barely be budged. Currently, they were opened to the township that bustled beyond. Haven looked to Leonardo and then to the scene before them, and smiling, dove into the fray.

The small city was a conglomeration of trees and constructed buildings, vendors selling their crafts from every nook that allowed enough space to sit or stand. A canopy of taller trees shrouded the place as a comforting ceiling. The streets acted as forest paths, looping around large structures and doubling back from whence they came. Within a few minutes, Leonardo became completely lost in the eccentric town, but Haven seemed to know exactly where she was going.

The sides of these streets were littered with elfin oddities. Small boys and girls in loose drapes and flower-dappled hair chased after faeries. In some cases Leonardo witnessed mischievous faeries chasing the children. The little creatures glowed in the midmorning light, their buzzing wings catching the sun's rays. Vendors were nestled in every area- fortune tellers, healers, herbalists, cooks, and bakers lines the paths, offering their trades. Leonardo felt himself being drawn in by a particularly lovely nymph who claimed she could give the best massages in all of the North. Haven caught her friend in the nick of time by his waistcoat and dragged him along.

"Now's not the time to be distracted, mister," Haven chided lightly, tugging at his clothes. "Besides, I've heard she pilfers away your coin when you're entranced by her hands."

Leonardo pursed his lips and let himself be led away. He looked at the girl beside him, amused by the transformation that had occurred in her expression. It seemed that the farther she moved from the palace, the lighter her countenance became. It was as if a burden was being lifted from her person, and she could lose herself in the busy market air.

"You really like it out here, don't you, princess?" Leonardo queried, gently brushing off her hand when they had turned a corner.

Haven shrugged, but her face said it all. "Everyone still knows who I am. I mean- look at me," she tugged at her black hair, which had been woven into a long braid. Hers was the darkest of all the fair heads that passed her by. "But outside the castle grounds, it doesn't seem to matter as much. I can lose myself in all of this and for once, I feel like I can forget who I am for a while." The princess smiled, sadness twinkling in her emerald eyes. But the moment passed and she walked on, leaving Leonardo to trail behind with his thoughts.

Haven beckoned Leonardo further, ducking under a curtain of ribbons that hung from a low-lying tree. Leonardo looked up to find that the entire tree was filled with objects- cracked vases, old pieces of armor, pots and bottles, drapes and fabric- every single one of them delicately woven with vines and leaves to make a home for faeries. The creatures were darting in and about, chattering with one another while hovering in mid-air. They stared down at Leonardo with equal curiosity as he looked up at them, but their attention darted back to their daily tasks and the elf was forgotten.

"There aren't nearly as many of those little guys around in the East," Leonardo observed, letting the ribbon slide through his fingers as he passed underneath them.

Haven nodded, waving up at the faeries. One broke away from the rest and hovered just above her index finger. "These woods are ancient. We have always shared our land with the faerie folk; they have been our companions for many centuries." Haven and the faerie smiled at one another before the creature darted away again.

In many of the conversations overhead in passing, Leonardo found that the common folk were whispering about the thunderclouds. There was also talk of the catastrophe at the Revival Ball the night before, which brought Leonardo to question the princess on the matter.

"Haven, has there been any news on the condition of our merchant victim?" He asked. "he was not in the greatest condition when we left his side last night." He recalled the bandages that needed continuous changing, and the struggles the healers were having with working on their human patient.

Haven huffed and shook her head at the matter, an indicator that she had indeed been updated. "His state is stable at the present," she began. "The healers managed to patch him up all right. But he lost a lot of blood, and his fingers were rubbed raw to the bone."

"And what of the prince's attacker?" Leonardo persisted. "Is he still detained under the edict of the Council?"

"Thankfully, no. My father ordered the merchant's release early this morning. Needless to say the Council was upset about that," the princess replied, turning down a smaller side street. The great white walls that surrounded the town were drawing closer. "The man would have been in a much more dire state if you hadn't stepped in, my fine friend." She gave him a sideways glance, an admiring one.

The knight thought back to the previous evening, recalling the bloodied human merchant and the attacker of prince Kohan. Instinctively, Leonardo had jumped out and disarmed the human who held the dagger by parrying it with one of his own. Almost immediately afterward he had to force the attacker to the ground and protect him from the surge of angry elves who were about to converge on him. After recovering from the initial shock of nearly being stabbed, Kohan rose and diffused the situation, hands raised high in a gesture of calming and of peace.

The ball wasn't quite the same after that; the human merchants were in a rage that one of their own had been so badly wounded. It took a lot of coaxing and calming from the prince and princess to finally cool everyone down. The two had been great ambassadors for the rest of the evening, tag-teaming and working with the humans, King Dromo, and the Council to sort everything out. Leonardo had been left to care for the traumatized woman who had collapsed to the floor. He never liked to see a lady cry; he took great lengths to ensure that she was comforted and relaxed. She thanked him many times for his concern, but he found himself more often than not staring across the room at the woman with her arm in a sling.

It later reached Leonardo what exactly had happened on the ballroom floor. The victim had been dancing with the elven maiden, and it appeared that she had gotten nervous with a gesture the man had made to her. Still, no one could be sure about what had actually happened- the woman refused to make mention on the topic- but she reacted with an outburst of magic that did not bode well for her partner.

It wasn't until very late at night that Leonardo had met up with Haven once more. The poor thing looked exhausted; he found that if she stood for too long, she would begin to sway like a fragile leaf in the wind. Leonardo guided her back to her bedchamber- the reliance she placed on him to walk straight concerned the knight. He had ordered her to go straight to bed, and she didn't refute him. Before turning to go, she rested her head on his chest again- as she had when they were dancing- and whispered a silent thank you. Leonardo lingered at her door several moments after she had closed it.

Leonardo shook himself from his reverie and directed his focus to Haven. "It was my honor and duty to protect our beloved prince," He thought for a moment, and laughed out right. "Do you believe that this will remove me from the good prince's list of nemeses?"

Haven chuckled with him. "I don't know, Leonardo. My elder brother truly knows how to hold a grudge."

At this point, the two friends had neared the outskirts of the village; many of the houses were residential and the streets were less crowded. The white fortress walls began to overshadow the streets; Leonardo looked up to find guards pacing about the top, and archers posted every twenty yards, constantly looking out over the Forrest.

Haven neared yet another gate, which towered higher than the iron gate and was comprised of solid metal.

"Those doors aren't opening any time soon," Leonardo observed, eyeing a large lock in the center of the glinting metal. He recalled just the other day entering through these gates with the rest of his troop, exhausted and road-weary.

"That's all right. We are going over the top," Haven grinned, leading him closer.

"I suppose we can accomplish this by vaulting?" he quipped, seeing no other options around.

Haven shook her head and sighed. "Just watch," she ordered, taking a step forward. Putting two fingers in her mouth, she whistled a tune. Putting a hand over her eyes to block the sun, she waited.

A rope ladder unfurled from the top of the wall and a knight appeared, waving down at Haven. She waved back and began to climb. Leonardo followed suit, and he soon became eye-level with the canopy of the trees.

A light wind ruffled his blonde hair upon standing on top of the great wall. As far as his eyes could see, the Royal Forrest stretched out before him, majestic and ancient. Leonardo could feel the old magic of the land rising from the trees; the air was thick with primeval power. It was hard for him to adjust to. The land of the East always had a blustering wind and the scent of the foaming sea in the air. Here, it was still and grand. The forest stretched up, covering the mountains to the West in a coat of fresh green foliage. The caps of the Petoac Mountains still held patches of snow, but rock was beginning to peek out from under its white blanket.

Leonardo found himself staring at the mountains. He wondered what it was like to explore the other side, what it was like to go into the Human realm. He had heard so many stories, about their barbaric living conditions and how they shrouded themselves in fire and smoke. There was nothing to truly confirm or deny these claims, but something in Leonardo moved him to discover what was true. Was it just as beautiful on the other side? He wondered. It had been so long since he had visited the Western Kingdom; that was as far as he had ever gone. Thinking on Eringoth's beloved outpost kingdom, Leonardo recalled the missing Western knight brigade with worry. The West had fallen into shadow, and no one had heard from the place in several days. Leonardo made a point to ask Haven if any news had been discovered since the previous evening.

Taking the ladder and carefully climbing down onto the other side of the wall, Haven and Leonardo landed on the lush forest floor. The ladder ascended again and the two were left to fend for themselves in the Royal Forrest.

Leonardo stared around in wonder. As the two walked to road on that led to the gate, Leonardo found himself gazing around at the lush green foliage that completely encased everything. Spring flowers had begun to sprout amongst the bushes and low trees, dangling from branches and peering up from the ground. The smell of damp earth was inhaled with every breath, as well as the humidity that wafted from drying leaves in the morning sun.

At a first glance, the forest seemed to lie perfectly still, and to an untrained eye it would remain eerily unmoving and silent. But the elves could see everything, hear everything that occurred under the shady trees. More faeries made their living out in the woods, but they were shyer and kept their distance from the traveling elves. They peeked out from nooks in trees, rounded, feral eyes staring curiously at their larger cousins.

Leonardo glimpsed a few nymphs and dryads gliding amongst the trees. While some carried the complexion of lime or olive, others held the hue of russet and chestnut. Their hair was a mass of vines and leaves of all varieties, and their eyes were a bright unearthly yellow. The creatures glided airily along, leaping over obstacles as a graceful deer would.

Leonardo called out to one, who stopped momentarily at hearing her own language leaving an elf's mouth. Haven stilled abruptly at hearing the strange wispy language flowing from her friend's tongue, and watched him with fascination. The nymph seemed intrigued; Leonardo asked her name. She seemed offended at the question and hissed before rejoining her friends and dancing off into the shadows.

Haven looked up at him, tickled. "It seems that you can't entertain a woman of another race as easily as you can for our own," she jabbed, patting him on the back.

Leonardo shrugged, smiling. "She declared that I was outshining her own beauty and therefore could not love me," he joked. "Their kind has a humor that is a little dry for me."

Haven chuckled at the joke and shook her head. "Come now, my odd friend. My secret is but a ways further."

The two had reached the road and continued along its path for a time. The sun had risen in the sky, and the morning chill had begun to give way to the warm spring day. Dew had evaporated from the ground, leaving the leaves all around to spring forth with new vigor. Leonardo was compelled to brush some of the leaves with his fingers as he passed them by.

Leonardo watched Haven inhale and exhale deeply; she seemed to unfurl and relax in the natural environment. Though one could never truly let their guard down in such a wild place, Leonardo could empathize with the girl. There was something about being pinned up in such formal structures that drew elves away from their true place with the land. While Leonardo and surely everyone else was glad for the protection they were provided, he found it nice to escape back to the Goddess's works.

"You can breathe easier out here," Haven said abruptly, as if she could read Leonardo's thoughts.

"Indeed," he mused. Haven, of all people, probably loved it out here best, simply because it didn't matter that human blood flowed in her veins. "The saplings and grass care not for who you are. They embrace you as the Goddess does, with peaceful acceptance."

"Or with apathy," Haven added. "Not that I particularly mind that, either. It is because of these things that I have led you out here, Leonardo." She paused on road and peered off into the woods. She strayed a ways from the path, feeling individual trunks and letting the grass at her feet glide between her fingers. Upon approaching a particularly gnarled tree, she beckoned that Leonardo come closer. "We have arrived," she smiled quietly, her hand running over the bark.

As Leonardo drew closer, he found that the trunk was covered with markings from the ancient tongue. They were branded into the bark with some form of magic, making the marks slightly raised and smooth above the rough bark. Small symbols accompanied the words, images that stood for peace and longevity, the Goddess and her children. Some markings had become overgrown with moss, but others seemed fresh and more recent. Leonardo was perplexed as to why these engravings were here, but by the look on Haven's face, he imagined that he would find out soon enough.

"Follow me," Haven whispered, green eyes gleaming as she descended into the shade of the trees.

The path was small and indiscernible at times, but Haven seemed to know where she was going. When she found that the knight was mildly perplexed as to the direction in which she was headed, Haven held out her hand behind her for Leonardo to take. Despite the emasculation he was sure to feel later, Leonardo did not refuse her. Her hand fit snugly into his own larger one. When she squeezed his palm he could feel his heart pump a little faster.

After walking for a time in silence, a clearing began to appear a little ways down the trail. Light shone through the boughs of the trees, casting unique shapes in the thick air before it hit the ground. The knight was forced to squint his eyes as they adjusted. There was a small stream that trickled into a pool at the center of the clearing, where reeds and stones cluttered its periphery.

Adjacent to the small pool was a single red maple tree and a pale stone that stood erected underneath.

Too soon, Haven released Leonardo's hand and walked ahead to where the stone protruded from the bosom of the earth. It was covered in moss and ivy, and the once sharp edges were dulled with weathering and time. Haven approached the stone and let her hand flow along the top, not quite touching the surface. The rock seemed to react to her proximity; it turned a rusty hue when her hand neared it and made a soft sizzling sound.

Leonardo neared the rock as well, curious. "A tomb? A magical one at that," he observed, not feeling comfortable with testing the spell for himself.

Haven nodded, her face hidden by her black locks. "It reacts whenever a relative is close by, but only the Goddess's hands can touch it. It helps to protect the obelisk." She fell silent for a while, staring at the gleaming stone. "This is my secret. I wanted to show you. My mother lies at our feet."

Leonardo was suddenly hit with the gravity of being taken to such a place. To his knowledge, no one knew where the human queen had been laid to rest, for she wasn't allowed to be interred in the royal graveyard. He felt his heart quicken in pace, not knowing exactly how to feel.

Almost without thinking, Leonardo bent to his knees and sat on his feet, hands laced in his lap. Haven followed suit but crossed her legs in front of her instead. The man inwardly shook his head; the princess was never one to follow regulation, for any sort of occasion.

Haven clasped her braid and began to stroke it thoughtlessly as she stared at the stone. Her visage had become rather somber, eyes pensive. Leonardo bowed his head respectfully to the grave, deciding to wait until the princess spoke.

"I don't know the ancient tongue very well, but I've memorized that the grave reads," she began, reaching out again to the stone where the encryptions lay. The same russet color concentrated where her fingers hovered closest to the stone. "'Here lies May Cendra, Queen of the Quartet Kingdoms of Eringoth. Her rule was brief, but the love she gave to her people and her family is timeless. She rests in the heavens with our Maker, a true lady warrior," Haven paused again, dropping her hand. The auburn hue dissipated and the stone was clean white once more. "On the nights that I couldn't sleep, for fear of the nightmares that I knew were awaiting me, I would chant those words to myself until I couldn't conceive another thought. 'Lady warrior…'" she repeated, almost to herself.

"Do you remember her?" Leonardo asked, feeling it appropriate to make eye contact with Haven now. He was beginning to realize that what he was hearing was rarely uttered aloud; he wouldn't have been surprised if this was the first time she had vocalized these thoughts.

Haven squinted at the stone, retreating to a place in her mind that Leonardo could not follow. "Just barely. It's not so much a face or a particular day, though I have been told that I look identical to her," Haven began twisting her braid between her fingers. She closed her eyes. "I recall a touch. Her hands on my face, then she kisses my forehead. Her fingers are so warm on my cheeks, like she's giving her life into me."

Leonardo nodded. ". She passed when you were a little lassie, if I recall correctly?" She had said something to him once before, but it was in passing.

"Yes. I was three years old. I don't remember the day, but the feeling of emptiness is still potent in my mind. The day she didn't come back." She paused, reflecting on the matter. Her voice was heavy and dry. At this point, she was more pensive than anything else- a train of thought so trodden that all the tears had already been shed. "It's so sad. I can't even remember what her voice sounds like. The color of her eyes."

The knight looked over at his friend, and tweaked her chin with his hand. "I'm sure they looked just like yours."

Haven smiled into her lap, but the grin faded and she fell into thought once more. She seemed to be pondering hard, attempting to recover memories that had been stolen from her by a thief that went by the name of Time.

"Do you know how she died?" Haven asked, still looking into her lap.

Leonardo thought. "You told me once before. On the day that I questioned you about the Royal family." He recalled. The girl he had interviewed on that day was not the woman that sat beside him now. His mind flashed back to several years ago, when he sat across from a girl in a lime green gown. The dress didn't fit her, and she had obviously been forced into it against her will. Some poor maid had tried to master the princess's hair, but it had become knotted and tangled with leaves from some outdoor adventure gone wrong.

A scowl seemed to be permanently fixed to the girl's face, her lower lip protruding ever so slightly in a youthful attempt at defiance. Those dark eyebrows were drawn together, as if a string had been sown tight between them. Even back then, Leonardo found the girl to be charming in her own eccentric way. There was a pride in her eyes that blazed fiercely, adding a glow about her.

The woman who sat beside Leonardo still held that confidence, but it was now tempered with a modesty that she had come to adopt over the years. She had matured, both emotionally and physically, and Leonardo was just coming to realize it in the manner of how she spoke of her deceased mother. There was a tempered logic to it all now, and though it was obviously still hard for the girl to express herself, there was an attempt to make it happen in the first place.

"Do you recall what I had told you?" She asked after Leonardo had fallen silent.

"Of course, though you were rather vague about it," he man replied, thinking back to his dissertation. "I had focused on the mystery behind her passing in my work. I made my own speculations, too. When you had told me that she had taken ill, there was not a doubt in my mind that it was at most a half-truth."

"That's the official story. The one that everyone found to be true, as it was written in the books that way," Haven muttered, a tinge of annoyance sparking in her tone.

"So the truth lies with her in the grave," Leonardo presumed, looking on at the stone.

Haven nodded. "And with her children and husband. We know, but few others do. It would trigger controversy if anyone found out."

Leonardo's interest was climbing. He found himself to be fixed on Haven's mouth, waiting for it to unveil the next thought that burdened her mind. "Controversy? What in the world happened, Haven?"

The princess huffed, looking up into the blue sky. Only a few clouds smeared themselves in soft wisps over the cerulean canvas. "The day my mother passed was in the mid spring of many years ago. Back in those days, she and my father loved to go for an afternoon ride in the Royal Forrest; it was a way for them to respite after a demanding day in the castle. Sometimes they would even hunt a fox or a deer. It was said that May Cendra always loved the chase. My father always said that she didn't have to chase after him for long though; he was quite spellbound by her when they first met." Haven smiled just then, reflecting.

"On the return from their ride in the woods, my father had noticed that my mother was riding her horse rather poorly, and it had become a struggle for her to remain upright on her mount. Upon returning to the castle and dressing down from the riding gear, they had found that a series of small darts had hit my mother in the arms and neck. From the little wounds dripped a yellow liquid," Haven bit her lip, obviously relaying the information from her father's perspective. His pain had subsequently been transferred to her own face. "They held some sort of deadly poison, one that slowed her bodily functions until it was hard for her to breathe. Her complexion had turned pale and her condition very quickly worsened. By the time the sun had fallen that day, she had breathed her last breath."

Another span of silence accompanied the final sentence. Not knowing how to react, Leonardo remained motionless, letting the forest around him fill in the quiet. He tentatively placed a hand on her shoulder. Almost mindlessly, the girl placed one of her own hands on top of his.

"My father's immediate thought was that it had been no accident," Haven continued after some time. "It was no secret that there were many elves in the North who abhorred the fact that their great king had chosen to wed a human. An investigation had been conducted, and it was found that the poisonous serum was elfin in origin. But the search ended there. My father knew that if he pursued the issue or made it public, the fallout would have been disastrous."

"Why?" Leonardo let the question slip out. He couldn't help but wonder.

"Our people would have felt betrayed by King Dromo if he turned on them and began accusing them of killing his wife, even if it was true. My mother's killer, if there even was one, probably had accomplices that would lie for him in the face of interrogation." Haven sighed, giving Leonardo's hand a little squeeze. "Besides. The last thing my mother would have wanted was for our kingdom to fall apart. The murderer would have gotten what he wanted if King Dromo went on a mad search for justice. So her death was played off as a severe illness and that was the end of everything."

"What do you think about all of this?" Leonardo asked, realizing how cold Haven's voice had become.

Haven's lip jutted out a tad, as it had back when Leonardo was interviewing her. "Honestly. I want to find my mother's killer and bring him to justice," her voice had become hard. "I know he is still here, in the kingdom. He must be. But no matter how much I want to seek him out, I know that I must keep the secret. For the sake of the kingdom," she trailed off for a moment, uncertainty crossing her face. "Sometimes I have dreams, Leonardo." The man next to her perked at the mentioning of his name. He peered into her face, which had become almost afraid. Her big eyes met his, and stayed there. "I have dreams about my mother. She comes to me, arms outstretched, trickling yellow blood. Her lips move and I try to listen to the words they create, but she is mute. The look she gives me," Haven shuddered involuntarily; her smaller frame quaking under her friend. Leonardo instinctively pulled her close.

"You know it's just a dream," Leonardo murmured, rubbing Haven's shoulder. She was becoming more and more worked up as she spoke.

"And you know what dreams are," Haven retorted, voice trembling. "The dead communicating with the living. My father seeks not to betray his people. But by sitting idly by and knowing the truth, I feel that I'm betraying the woman who gave birth to me." Haven's lips pursed together again, and she angrily swatted at a tear before it could make a track down her cheek.

In situations like these, Leonardo usually knew what to say. There was always a line that would do the trick, a joke that could make the girl crack a smile. If he was bold enough, he could wipe away a tear. But not this time. He sat, perplexed at his own helplessness as the girl under his arm battled with her own worries. There was something inconsolable here, that if addressed would sound forced or insincere. So the knight opted to hold his tongue and wait for Haven to console herself.

But a question did enter Leonardo's mind, one that had been taking form in his conscious mind for quite some time. He didn't know if it was appropriate to ask such a thing, but his pressing curiosity eventually led him to speak. "Why are you telling me all of this?" he asked softly, once Haven's breathing had steadied. The quiet that hung in the air held so many possible answers.

Haven glanced up at him and sniffed, thinking. "Out of all the people that I know, and out of everyone that I live with in the North, no one quite understands me like you do. I don't know what it is about you, but even despite your ornery nature and all of your shenanigans, I know that…I can trust you." By the end, her rosy lips had curled into a smile.

Leonardo felt that there were horses' hooves galloping against his ribcage, and a color had risen in his cheeks, looking as if he had too much mead to drink. All he could muster without making a fool of himself was, "I'm honored, princess. Truly."

In that moment, his face was indescribably close to hers. For the second time in under twenty four hours- an unquestionable want began to ensnare Leonardo's thoughts. It would be so easy; all he would have to do is cup her narrow face in his hands. He found himself wanting to pull a wisp of hair out of her eyes, so that he could see them more clearly. There was such pain in them; Leonardo wanted nothing more than to make that hurt go away. It could be so easy. He would just close his eyes, and lean in.

A rustling in the woods beyond the clearing pulled Leonardo from his deepening train of thought. He exhaled sharply and ran a hand through his flaxen hair; he truly hoped the princess under his arm hadn't become aware of his fast-beating heart. Looking around, he eyed the forest, listening again for the noise echoing from the branches. Quite a ruckus was being made; in the distance a flock of birds was seen fleeing from the trees, squawking in irritation. There was a snap of a branch and the ensuing rustling of leaves- whatever was drawing near certainly was not being subtle about it.

"I'm not the only one who hears that, I hope," Leonardo muttered. His ears involuntarily pricked as the rustling became louder and more distinct.

Haven tensed up, releasing Leonardo's hand. It had taken her a little longer to locate the noise, a result of her human ears. Out of habit, her hand went to the jeweled sheath at her hip, where a six inch dagger lay waiting for her summons. "What in the world could it be," she questioned, unable to identify the creature by its footsteps.

The two friends stood; Haven instinctively put herself between whatever was approaching and her beloved mother's tomb. Leonardo followed suit. He hadn't brought a weapon with him- a mistake he was inwardly scolding himself for- but prepared to call any animal allies he may need if a confrontation was to ensue.

"O, wandering one! This is land blessed by the Goddess. What brings you to this sacred place?" Haven called out, her voice crisp and filled with power.

There was no reply, which lead Haven and Leonardo both to crouch in preparation for a confrontation. One could never be too cautious of the animals that inhabited these woods. The snapping of twigs became louder and more defined; soon enough the shadow of a figure began to materialize in the dim of the woods. The creature had a stumbling gait, as if it had some deformity or limp.

"Who goes there?" Haven yelled again, her voice becoming increasingly foreboding. She was not letting anything happen to her mother's burial ground.

Leonardo's eyes widened, and he stayed Haven as she was about to advance. "It's a person," he realized, eyeing the figure.

Haven squinted into the dim; she was having trouble seeing the outline in the cover of the trees. "Are you sure?"

Before Leonardo could confirm it, the person shed the cloak of the forest and stumbled out into the clearing.

It was a man, bruised and battered. His tunic was torn by brambles and cut by what seemed like sword slashes- his pants were in similar condition. The man came into the light and was almost immediately blinded by it- an arm flew up to cover his eyes. A necklace glinted at the man's neck in the sunlight; it left chafed red skin all about his collar. Leonardo most immediately noticed the hue of the man's hair. It was a deep dark navy color, but shone in the light in such a manner that betrayed other shades of blue, and was most certainly elfin. Upon discerning the color of the elf's hair, Leonardo bit back a gasp.

It couldn't be.

The man looked up at the two who guarded the grave. His eyes were wide blue discs; he was evidently as surprised as the other two were at seeing elves out in the forest. He stumbled forward, approaching the two with an air of desperation. He tried to speak, but his parched throat and exhausted vocal chords only allowed a groan to escape. It seemed as if his legs had decided to cease working- as soon as the man tried to walk any further he collapsed to the ground.

Leonardo and Haven looked at one another, then at the figure crumpled in the green grass. They rushed toward the elf together, the same fear gripping their hearts.

Seven

KOHAN

THE CASTLE CORRIDORS LAY SILENT in the mid-morning. A single page's boots could be heard, echoing down hall after hall, without any other interruption. The windows that faced the sun flooded the halls with a brilliant orange glow. Marble walls glistened, their churning patterns doused in the warm hues of daylight. Mornings after the Revival were commonly expected to remain ghostly, and that day was no exception. Elves danced until the orchestra could play no more and the magical orbs that floated in the air were drowned out by the natural aura of the sun.

On any other Revival, the prince of Eringoth would sleep in with the rest of his kingdom and take the morning to recover from the celebration. However, when he emerged from his bedchamber, it was quite clear that no sleep had been acquired in the previous night.

Kohan had stripped off the ceremonial armor from the ball, but continued to wear the shimmering velvet maroon tunic and cream colored trousers that rested underneath. He had tried to bat out the creases with his hands, but it was to little avail. Instead, he trudged down the hallway, attempting to tame his hair, which had gone through numerous hand-rakings and ruffling from distressed thought.

No sleep was in line for this prince, especially after the attempt on his life was made and there was still the question of the Western Knights to be solved. The previous evening had been spent interrogating the merchant who had attacked him with the blade- the prince made a personal note to thank Sir Leonardo later.

Despite Kohan's personal qualms with the Eastern scholar-turned-knight, he was grateful for the man's act of loyalty.

Kohan's princely duties had overwhelmed him that evening, preventing him from reveling in the celebrations. He spent many hours delegating between the enraged humans who demanded their comrade to be released, and the ancient counselors who declared that an instant hanging was the only solution to the issue at hand. Kohan silently cursed humanity for their primeval drives- if the merchant hadn't been so forward with the elf maiden, none of this would have happened.

Between this and needing to make time to consult with King Dromo, Kohan found himself unable to attend to his Lady Moira throughout the night. At first he was grateful for Ailill's intervention with ensuring her comfort, but his gratitude had thinned as time wore on and he found Ailill becoming a little too comfortable with the woman in the blue dress.

The prince tramped down the hall from his bedchamber, the light shining in his face was an unwelcome present from the Goddess that morning. As attendants and maids passed him by, Kohan fixed his posture and let his princely mask do the small conversation. When he was alone again, he let himself crumple, stretching out his tired muscles.

He reached into his pocket and withdrew a creased note- he opened the frayed parchment and reconfirmed the time inscribed on it. The letters sloped in elegant penmanship, with thin black lines that stood out like cuts in the paper:

"Eight o'clock. As the rivers run red, so will the sky with our unabated rage."

Kohan nodded, pondering over the phrase as he took his usual route into the bowels of the palace. His bedchambers rested in the higher regions of the building; Kohan had to traverse many flights of stairs to finally reach the ground floor where the grand entrance hall, throne room, dining areas, libraries and ballroom all resided. He then continued onward, swiping an apple from a page's tray as he passed, and ducked into a side-corridor near the medical bay.

He descended one flight of stairs after another. The prince had to pause momentarily before continuing on- the constant circling and following stone pattern after another was making his head spin.

Upon opening yet another door, Kohan felt the chill of the underground begin to seep into his clothing. A dampness clung to the air and torches had to assist the small natural light that peeked in from skylights in the ceiling. The air smelled of freshly growing moss; he turned to the side and found small patches of the plant growing on the walls and corners of the floor. It glowed dimly in the corridor's light, colors of lime and rose and cream. A smile spread onto Kohan's face- no doubt one of Dromo's attempts to bring the forest to the castle.

The roar of the waterfall that abutted the North side of the castle became more distinct the farther Kohan plunged into the corridor. It was a constant hissing; he could feel the force of the falls battering the side of the castle and a slight humming could be discerned if he touched the walls.

Kohan had been down this path frequently enough, but few others were even allowed into this part of the castle. They either knew they were forbidden to enter or had no knowledge of its existence at all. The prince felt for the keys in his breast pocket, knowing he would need them as soon as the red door came in sight.

Soon enough he had found it, the painted wood nestled in with the darkened wet stone. Kohan let a hand run over the smooth surface, the potent scent of magic leaving the surface as his fingers parted with it. The prince withdrew a little golden key no larger than his own thumb, and placed it into the equally glistening doorknob.

Before turning the key, Kohan waited for the door to respond. Previously, where there had been only red paint before, black etchings began to carve themselves in the wood. The markings coalesced together to form a query for the prince.

"What do the clouds carry for us, firstborn Ibis?"

Kohan smirked. Dromo was always coming up with clever way to address his son. Ibis was a new one, probably t a reference to his claret eyes. The prince closed his eyes and muttered the phrase he was given in the note in ancient tongue. The words slithered from his mouth, laden with magic that seemed to fall from his lips in a misty white breath. The mistiness seeped into the door around the black markings.

The door seemed to stand there, contemplating Kohan's response to its question. As quickly as the etchings had appeared, they healed themselves back into the wood and the door became completely red once more. Kohan then turned the lock and let himself inside.

Kohan flinched at the white light that consumed him upon entering the room. His footsteps echoed into the high ceiling above him as he rubbed his eyes with a moan. "I still struggle with becoming accustomed to such a transition, my Lord," he murmured, stalking into the open space.

"You know how I love the light, my son," Dromo replied from the chair on the far side of the room, his silver hair spilling over the back of it.

Kohan's eyes adjusted to the natural light that surrounded them. The wall on the far side of the room was made completely of glass and carried a full frontal view of the waterfall outside. The room was situated at the base of the falls, and there was a constant turmoil outside the muted room. Dromo had long ago cast a spell that could shut out the din of the falls, as to preserve the peace of this space. Kohan let his eyes wander to the ceiling above, which was nothing more than a cave roof of stalagmites colored in rainbows of reds, oranges, creams and navy blues. From the tips of the spiked rocks hung all manner of wind chimes and bells. These talismans twanged and tinkled when Kohan passed under them, their shiny organic bodies reflecting the movement of the waterfall outside.

Kohan passed stacks of ancient books that littered floors and tables, texts bookmarked with all manner of quills and ribbons spilling onto the carpet. The otherwise orderly king never cared much for the condition of his study.

"I hope I'm not too late," Kohan began, approaching his father. A portrait of the Royal Family hung on one of the other cave walls. The eyes of the four family members from a time gone by seemed to follow Kohan as he passed by.

The King of Eringoth shook his head. "I filled the time with my own thoughts. No need to apologize. But there are pressing matters at hand that need to be addressed." Dromo stood, facing his son. He placed a trinket he had been fiddling with on the table at his side. It was a turquoise flower hairpin- Kohan could only guess it was another one of May's belongings that the king couldn't part with.

"I hear that you released mister Winchester at sunrise," Kohan said, stroking his chin. He was at war with himself on the issue. It is not a very good feeling when someone wants you dead.

"Our friend was under a grave misunderstanding. You know this," Dromo stated, striding across the room to look out the glass wall. "He was looking out for his kinsmen, as any of us would have done in his shoes."

Kohan rolled his eyes- he really hoped his father didn't notice. "I do believe an elf would have better assessed the situation before charging an innocent man and threatening his life."

"We must give these people a chance, my son," Dromo glanced over at Kohan. His eyes had hardened from hours of thought. There were noticeable creases under his lids from sleep deprivation and stress. "There is good at their core. I have seen it. Both our races could benefit greatly from mutual interaction."

Kohan sighed. The fact that there had indeed been a violent incident had greatly disheartened the king. It had taken weeks of battling the Council to invite them before the elders even considered it. Now it would seem that it would take months for the topic to even reach the table again.

"What if one of the humans decided to become violent again?" Kohan pressed, irritation tickling his thought. "We need to think of our people as well, my lord. Before, they were skeptical but willing to participate. Now many are becoming angry with these attempts at forging bonds that were not meant to be made." A small voice inside Kohan's head was telling him to stop speaking. But he held his ground, fists balling together as irritation prickled his cheeks.

Dromo examined Kohan, sweeping his eyes up and down his figure. The King folded his arms with an air of understanding, chin lifted toward the heavens. A chill leaked into his voice. "You mean to say that my efforts are futile. That I am wasting the labors of both my people and my son."

Kohan drew himself to his full height, inhaling his own annoyance. "I mean to say that our kin should be the first priority, my lord." 'Lord' came with a slight sting at the end. "We are dealing with elements that could quite easily spiral out of our control." He knew that a confrontation was the last thing that either of them needed, but this had to be said.

"This is precisely why I need you by my side, prince Kohan. If we are going to integrate our people and forge a connection to communicate ideas, I need the assistance of my best man." Dromo pressed, relenting a little in hopes to relax the prince. He let his arms fall to his side.

"What is this all for, anyway?" Kohan asked suddenly, not completely internalizing what Dromo had said. "What ideas are worth exchanging? I can't imagine humans have much to offer in ways that outmatch our own."

Dromo's eyes softened a little, his jaw slacked. "It is not about the technology, or the ideology, prince Kohan. It is a state of mind."

"That one should jump to conclusions and take violent action?" Kohan grunted, shifting his weight onto one foot. He crossed his arms over his chest. "Knee-jerk reactions are certainly something that a society could use more of."

Dromo sighed and shook his head. He passed his son for a few paces, hovering near his desk again. "We teach them to temper their emotions. And they give us the capacity to feel. There is a balance that is meant to be between our two races, I can feel it in my bones."

"It won't bring her back, father." Kohan broke in, his voice softening just a little. The anger had subsided into bitterness. "Dragging more humans into Eringoth will not fill the void that she left."

Dromo had gone rigid, emotions churning beneath the surface gave way to a completely immobilized form. His eyes had dropped to the desk; hands making their way back to the hairpin. He toyed with the trinket, watching it glint in the sunlight as he exchanged it between his fingers.

Kohan watched his father uncomfortably, realizing what exactly he was saying. "She, too was human. But she was not just any human, father." He added, fearful to approach the great man, but wanting to rescind all the bitterness that had fallen from his lips.

The king slowly shook his head, as if attempting to dispel the negativity floating around him. "If you think so depressingly on humans, what hope do you have for your half- sister?"

Kohan stopped, falling as still as his father.

"Kohan, I still cannot discern your personal philosophy on humans. But, for the love of the Goddess, do not speak to Haven in this way. Her blood may carry both human and elfin elements, but no matter your thoughts, think on her as your kin and as your sister."

"I always have," Kohan muttered, almost to himself, looking at his hands. He thought of Haven and became immediately ashamed. In his anger he had inadvertently lashed out at his own sister.

"Then let us not dwell on these things. We can revisit the condition of mister Winchester and his friend in the medical bay later in the evening," Dromo said abruptly, the broken expression on his face becoming remolded into the mask of a ruler. His lips had been drawn into a thin line; he gestured for Kohan to stand opposite him at the desk.

Kohan stood tall, but recognized an order when he saw one and stood where he was directed.

"There are more pressing issues at hand that I summoned you to discuss," Dromo continued, unfurling a large scroll so that it covered the expanse of his mahogany desk. A map of Eringoth spread out before them. His voice was strictly business-like; Kohan avoided looking into his eyes. "As you may well know, the Western Kingdom has fallen into shadow. There has been no formal contact from the kingdom for several days now. No messages, people, transit, goods, anything have left the kingdom. Our mages have struggled to contact their counterparts in the West as well, to no avail. This is extremely concerning."

"In addition to the missing cavalry, it is especially so," Kohan let himself say. Every word was guarded, as if attempting to make up for the multitude of slips prior. A thought struck him. "Have you tried contacting Lord Ronan with your crystal?"

Dromo reached to the red crystal that rested on a small golden necklace. It fit snugly in the palm of his hand, oval in shape, and held the color of a dying sunset. Kohan knew that each of the four kings owned an Enthima crystal- a gem that could directly contact any of the other rulers.

The king's eyes were shaded. He looked at the crystal before he let it fall from his grasp. "It was no use. The connection was cut."

Kohan was perplexed. A seed of fear had planted itself in his stomach, a dark little pit that made him feel sick. "What does that mean?"

"If King Ronan has been divorced from his crystal, the implications are…severe." Dromo looked away, leaning forward so that his hands rested on the desk. "I have already notified the other kings. They are just as perturbed as I am."

"Someone could use the crystal to see the other three kings," Kohan speculated, running a hand through his wine-colored hair. "There's no way he simply could have lost it, correct?"

"Never," Dromo muttered, his ominous tone betraying a fear that made Kohan shiver. "And it fits all too well with the disconnection from the entire kingdom. I can only guess that the necklace has been stolen, or King Ronan has been... compromised."

The very thought draped itself heavily over the two elves. Its effect seemed to dim the room. "What is happening over there," Kohan asked himself, letting his finger trace over the Petoac Mountains on the map until it rested on the depiction of a small black tower. He tapped it twice, hoping in vain that the little black drawing would answer all of his questions.

"It is precisely because we have no knowledge of what is happening that we must act at once. I have begun to assemble a small brigade to make the trek into the West," Dromo declared, taking a small rod and tapping the location of the Northern Kingdom.

"Our mages can assemble a spell of some sort to do reconnaissance prior to their departure," Kohan suggested, eyeing the small thin path that led from the North to the West. "That way they can be prepared for anything upon entering the mountains."

Dromo nodded. "More research will have to be done- the merchants should most definitely be interviewed, to see if anything suspicious was happening in the region."

"I shall consult any and all of the merchants, if that pleases you," Kohan offered. He and his father worked better as a team. Antagonism in the family was the last thing that they needed.

The king glanced up at Kohan for a quick moment, with what seemed like gratitude flickering under the surface. "That will do very nicely," he said, voice remaining fairly solemn. "Collect Sir Gideon for that task as well. I believe he will be a useful implement to work with the merchants."

Kohan nodded, internalizing his orders. "That is the first object I will attend to when this meeting is adjourned."

"Ah, ah," Dromo waved his hand against Kohan's statement. "The next task I am prescribing for you is a good rest.

You have done a great deal for your kingdom in the past twenty four hours. Now you must do a service to yourself, and to your father."

Kohan met Dromo's gaze fully this time; there was a consensus between them that settled Kohan's heart a little. They shook hands over the desk in a firm grip. Kohan was about to turn on his heel to go, but he stopped himself. He looked at his father one final time. "Father, do you have any idea what is happening?"

Dromo took in his son and then looked out the glass wall once more. The waterfall pounded on the lake below, noiseless but terrifying in its own way. "There is no rightful explanation as to what events are taking place in our sister kingdom, but there are unnatural workings here that must be identified. I can only pray to the Goddess that the answers will come soon."

Kohan bowed, receiving a head-nod from Dromo in return, and left the study. He locked the door behind him, sealing the king and his thoughts back inside. There was no telling how long Dromo would remain in the study; sometimes he would vanish for hours at a time, contemplating his past and his kingdom.

Kohan swept from the bowels of the castle and returned to the main floor, which had become busier as the mid-morning wore on. The majority of the people were still attendants and servants, seeing that their masters and mistresses had a pleasant breakfast in bed or a warm bath. Kohan received bows and salutations wherever he went, and when the prince would normally reciprocate the genial greetings, he remained silent and only gave a nod.

He was half-willing himself to go seek out Sir Gideon and begin interviewing the humans anyway when the choice had already been made for him. While walking past the throne room, which rested just behind the entrance hall, Kohan heard himself being hailed from across the corridor. He turned in mild surprise to see Gideon jogging toward him. Like the prince, Gideon had removed his armor but still wore the ceremonial undergarments from the night before.

The elf approached Kohan, out of breath. His hair had been swept back from running and his cheeks were flushed. "My good prince," he gasped, wiping his forehead.

"Good Goddess, what is it, Captain?" Kohan queried, bemused at his comrade's state. "Why are you rushing about the castle like a mad boar?"

"It's that sister of yours," Gideon breathed. The mentioning of Haven immediately pricked Kohan's attention. "She's done it again."

Kohan grabbed Gideon's shoulder, steadying the man. "Is she all right? What has happened?"

Gideon gave an exhausted nod. The concerned knot that was forming in Kohan's chest uncoiled. "But you know how she's always getting into something. This time she's found a man in the Royal Forrest."

Kohan rubbed the bridge of his nose. "Why was she out in the middle of the Forrest," he murmured to himself. Of all the things she could be doing.

Gideon gave a shrug, thinking the question was meant for him. "I'm not rightly sure, but that's not even the strangest part. She's gone and found herself a Western prince."

Kohan turned to stare incredulously at the Captain of the Guard. His mouth dropped wide open. It couldn't be.

Eight
HAVEN

THERE WAS TOO LITTLE TIME to bring the man back down into the medical bay; his wounds were severe. It was a struggle to bring him from the forest through the town and into the castle. Crowds had gathered to watch the man be carried by Haven and Leonardo- the task was difficult, but Haven felt the burning need to accomplish it when she found that civilians were watching. Eventually, several palace guards had come down to meet them and Haven relented the stranger to their care.

Haven and Leonardo had doggedly trailed the man, however, ensuring that he did not leave their sight. They both felt responsible in some odd sort of way- having found him they wanted to make sure he was properly cared for. Up the entrance staircase to the castle, into the entry hall and off to a study lounge at the side was where they finally decided to rest the wounded man. The study was immediately quarantined. Sir Gideon, who had met Haven at the stairs and heard a brief story, went about shooing away onlookers and swept off in search of the prince.

Medical staff swirled around the fallen elf like a cyclone, pitching drapes to hide him from sight and bringing herbs and vials of medicine for his care. Soon enough the entire place had become an on-site operation for the elf. Curtains were drawn and the man was completely hidden from sight; the clinks of medical tools could be heard from beyond the cloth.

Haven was told that she should leave the area, but she remained, despite their sour looks. Leonardo sat by her side on a plush velvet couch and waited with her. From where they rested, they could only see the back of the couch on which the unconscious man laid. Maidens draped in white crowded over the couch, carrying bandages and salves.

Haven turned to her friend, who had been exhaling with fatigue. "You say this man is a prince, correct?"

The knight stretched back and looked up at the ceiling. "Indeed. A Western prince. You don't see that hue of hair anywhere else in Eringoth than in the Western Royal Family."

Haven sat, brooding for a moment. She wondered how in the world a prince managed go get so battered and lost in the middle of the Royal Forrest.

"There are only two princes that hail from the West," Leonardo continued. "And I've met the younger one before. I do believe that it is he who is in this room with us as I speak."

They both glanced over to the couch across from them. A pale hand was getting its pulse taken by one of the Healers clad in white.

Haven looked at Leonardo. "You've met him before?" She had wondered why such a puzzled expression had crossed his face upon seeing the man stumble from the woods.

"Yes. Once, when I was a younger lad on a courtly appearance with my father, the Duke. We were much smaller back then, but one never forgets such stunning hair," Leonardo smirked, recalling the distant past. "It was my first appearance at court as a fledgling member of my father's clan. There he was, Prince Aaren. No older then I, peeking out from his mother's royal gown. He seemed a reserved young boy, but what was he compared to me?"

"Everyone is reserved in comparison to you, my good friend," Haven teased, nudging his arm.

Leonardo snorted and continued on. "I had the chance to speak with him when all of the adults were chatting amongst themselves. Aaren seemed mildly intimidated by my openness- I was always looking to make new friends- but he warmed up to me eventually. For the rest of his stay in the East we were together. He was a good young man. Every word he spoke had a purpose."

Haven nodded, taking everything in. "So you're friends?"

"Not exactly. I haven't seen him since he left the Eastern Kingdom all those years ago. Our respective homes aren't exactly close. We kept in contact via letter when we could, but being a prince he was quite the busy one." The knight replied, speaking matter-of-factly.

Haven turned back to look at the couch. She matched the name with his face, his past with the one Leonardo described. But she wanted to know more. "He's certainly mysterious," she murmured, almost to herself.

"Why sit and watch him be tended to? There is nothing more we can do," Leonardo started, sagging into the couch. He had stopped listening to Haven's ponderings; it was obvious that he either wanted food or rest.

Haven stretched her shoulder by moving it in circles in its socket- she had really overused it in the process of carrying the elf. "He might not be awake right now, but I feel responsible for his hospitality. As a princess, it is my duty to tend to him. Besides, I can't help but think he'll wake with a start again like he had earlier."

While walking through the town below the castle, prince Aaren had jolted from unconsciousness and began to stumble through broken ancient tongue. He was incoherent and wild, using what was left of his strength to try and break free from the grasp of Haven and Leonardo.

"He only calmed himself when I spoke to him," Haven recalled softly. Looking back, his hand gripped the back of her neck in near desperation. His large cerulean eyes struck her. They were almost steely in nature; cold and filled with fear at the exact same time. He was trying to tell her something with that stare, something she simply could not identify. Part of her wanted to figure it out.

"There was something that calmed his nerves," Leonardo relented, puckering his lips in thought. Half his mind probably still lingered on food.

Haven was about to tell Leonardo to be excused so he could indulge himself, but Kohan arrived on the scene, perking everyone's interest. The prince drew back the curtains and stepped into the area near the couch, speaking with one of the Healers. His forehead was creased in thought as the woman whispered in his ear. Giving a quick nod, he left the drapes and strolled toward Haven and Leonardo. The two stood and bowed to the prince.

"Well. Prince Aaren has been greatly wounded, with lacerations, bruises, and cuts all about his person. Nothing seems to be broken, but healing will take a while," Kohan paused to catch his breath. "Sir Gideon tells me that it was you two who found Prince Aaren," Kohan started, not wasting a word. Haven noted the dark skin under his eyes and the creases of exhaustion formed at the edges of his mouth. Her poor brother seemed to be at the end of his rope.

"Yes, my lord," Leonardo affirmed.

"And I hear that you discovered him in the Royal Forrest. Pray tell, little sister, what were you doing out there?" Kohan directed his attention to Haven, who shrunk back at her brother's tone.

"I was visiting family," she returned guardedly, head lowered but eyes watching her brother's face.

Kohan seemed to crumple a little, irritation leaving his form. "Forgive me. I should have known," he sighed, rubbing his temples with his hand.

Haven went and kissed her brother on the cheek. She held part of his face in the palm of her hand. "It's all right, Kohan. Things have been a little out of sorts as of late."

"Truer words have not been spoken," Kohan grimaced. "And the appearance of a prince so far from his home in such condition is greatly unsettling. Has he said anything to you?"

Leonardo shook his head, feeling it acceptable to speak. "He was incoherent and restless when he was conscious. The man seemed to be pretty disturbed. By what, no one can be sure."

Kohan's expression continued to fall.

"What is it, brother?" Haven queried, concerned by this reaction.

"Contact me immediately when he awakens. I gather that Prince Aaren will have all of the answers for us when he does," Kohan stated, preparing to go on his way once more. He turned back and gave a nod in Leonardo's direction. "For last night, I owe you one, Sir Leonardo. You make a better knight than a scholar any day."

A smile broke across Leonardo's face. "I suppose you could start by ordering a warm meal to my quarters. I'm famished," Haven grinned in spite of herself.

Kohan rolled his eyes in good jest. "I shan't bring it to you, but I'll direct you to the kitchens for an early lunch."

Leonardo's eyes lit up and he prepared to follow the prince. "Haven, will you make a happy knight happier and revel in my company?"

Haven considered the fact, but shook her head and went back to sit on her couch. "I'd prefer to stay here, in case the prince wakes again. He might want to see a familiar face." She watched the light leave the knight's leaf-green eyes and felt a pang of guilt. "I'm sorry. I'll be here later if you want to stop by."

Leonardo fixed his small ponytail, a grin forced to resurrection. "No worries, princess. I'll bring you a little something later, if that pleases you."

"I'll gladly take whatever you haven't already eaten," Haven smiled back.

The two men bid Haven adieu and walked from the study. As they left, Haven heard Kohan telling Leonardo that the food favors wouldn't last long if he was so persistent. Leonardo turned the corner laughing; even Kohan had the semblance of a smile dancing on his tired lips.

Haven curled up on the couch, looping her good arm around her legs. A part of her was grateful to be alone again. All she expected this morning was to take a peaceful stroll in the

Forrest and she had gotten much more than that. It was nice to be able to rest with her thoughts.

The Healers just beyond whispered quietly, assessing the wounds of the prince before them. Their voices waded gently through the air, entering Haven's ears as indiscernible lullabies. She watched their faces, angelic and pale, as they worked, gauging their reactions to how well the healing was going. The process was slow but seemed to be going well. A pile of used bandages stained with red had begun to accumulate at the foot of the couch. A soft blue glow would occasionally rise from the slumbering figure, an indication of more wounds being closed.

The day wore on and the Healers worked in shifts, every couple of hours new elves would come in and the old guard would depart for nourishment and rest. Twice, Haven arose to ask the Healers if they needed any assistance. The first time, they had her run simple errands, like fetching new gauze and bandages or preparing a salve to apply to the wounds. When Haven could get in close enough, she was able to catch a glimpse of the fallen prince- bare chested and wrapped in bindings. His chest rose and fell softly and ever so slightly- if one had looked at him fleetingly they would have presumed him dead. Haven felt her cheeks reddening and she excused herself to return to the couch on which she rested.

Later in the late afternoon, Haven approached the Healers once more to see if they required any more help. Instead of giving her a task, they began to inspect her own arm and scolded her for not applying the ointment they had given her the previous day. So Haven found herself ensnared for a good quarter of an hour as the Healers momentarily focused on her shoulder. The healing seemed to be going well; the maidens simply warned Haven against carrying any more unconscious princes for the time being.

Now disgruntled and sporting an irritated shoulder, Haven returned to the couch, motivated not to rise again anytime soon. The falling sun cast long shadows in the study, lighting the books that lined the walls on fire and accenting the reds and golds that were laced in the carpet at her feet. The discarded rags, now placed in a basket, also burned with the dried liquid they held, an ominous glow.

Before long, with the combination of exhaustion and the soothing voices of the Healers, Haven found herself drifting off to sleep. She struggled to stay awake, but the comfort of the soft couch soon lulled her into its depths. Lying on her side, Haven let her black hair spill from its braid and cascade over the side of the couch's arm in a black waterfall. With her view still fixed on the couch across from her, Haven's eyes drew shut.

When she opened them again, the study room had fallen dark.

Haven blinked, adjusting her eyes to the dim. Torches and candles had been lit and the room was fairly well illuminated, but many of the healers had left. The drapes remained in place, however, and it seemed that the individual occupying the couch still rested there.

The princess forced herself to sit; her arm had grown stiff from lying in the same place for so long. Rubbing the muscles on her arm and grumbling under her breath, Haven wondered exactly how long she had slept. A small plate of bread and cheese rested on the floor beside her; she grinned and made a note to thank Leonardo later. She rose and swiped up the bread, cracking her back, and strode over to the sleeping man. Knowing she wasn't exactly allowed near him, she waited until a maiden had fetched the rags and left the study before she approached any further.

For the first time in hours she got a good glimpse at prince Aaren when she rounded the couch to face him. Drawing up an ottoman, Haven plopped beside the prince. Surrounding firelight danced on his cheeks, which were gaunt from many days of restless travel. His eyelashes were just as navy as the hair on his head. The elf's lips were slightly parted, and soft, content breaths traveled past them. Even in sleep, his eyebrows were tensed with trouble, as if any moment he would awake from a terrible dream.

The wounds on his chest had been bandaged tight, and no dressings needed to be changed as far as Haven could tell. His shirt rested on the back of the couch, bloodied and torn from the wilds of the forest.

Haven's eyes traveled to the necklace that clung to prince Aaren's collar. She tilted her head, befuddled at its alien composition, and could almost smell the potent magic that rolled from it. The skin around the necklace had been worn raw; ribbon of pink cut through his pale flesh. Some healing salves had been applied, which stopped most of the irritation, but it was clear that the trinket was an uncomfortable burden.

The sudden urge to touch the metal plates overwhelmed Haven's sense of judgment. She wanted to know what they felt like as she watched the little squares glow coolly in the candlelight. The heavy aura that emanated from the plates was enchanting to a point where her eyes couldn't leave them. Haven gingerly reached out her hand, letting her index finger stroke a plate that rested just above the prince's trachea.

Almost as immediately as the action had been taken, the prince bolted awake. He snatched at the wrist that had been near his neck and gripped on to it with incredible strength. Haven yelped in surprise and tried to yank away, but the man had firmly latched himself to her. Their eyes met- his were wide and wild. He took her in with a matter of seconds, eyes running up and down her facial features. The prince tried to speak again, frantic in his discourse, but the words only spilled out in the ancient tongue once more.

Recovering from the initial shock, Haven steeled herself and attempted to gain control over her rapidly beating heart. She shook her head, hushing and grabbing Aaren's other hand.

"Prince Aaren. My lord, I'm sorry. I can't understand you. You are safe here," she finished, breathing hard from the physical struggle. Her eyes locked onto his. Haven wasn't sure if he could understand what she was saying, but her gentle manner and sincere gaze nullified the prince's fears.

Prince Aaren seemed to internalize the words. His grip slackened and he crumbled back onto the couch, his burst of strength having ended. Haven watched his ribcage heave up and down as the man struggled to compose himself. His eyes had shut and his neck craned away, shying from the light.

Haven watched the man in silence for a few minutes, unsure of what to do. After a while, she thought that perhaps he had fallen back asleep. Guilt and confusion coursed through her. *Stupid, curious girl*, she scolded herself.

Haven resolved to rise and tell a Healer about what had happened- she really didn't want him to inflict any more wounds upon himself. As she moved to go, the prince sprung to life, this time grabbing her hand.

"Not yet," he whispered. Haven could feel a tremor rumble through his body. "The night is not kind to me."

Puzzled, Haven returned to her ottoman and readjusted her hand in his. "What can I do for you, my lord?" she asked sincerely.

The semblance of a smirk flickered across his face. "You may start by calling me Aaren. I hate formalities." His voice floated to her ears, a ghost's murmur.

Haven obliged with a nod. "Aaren it is."

Aaren studied her for a long while. He seemed to be more in his faculties now that the initial shock of consciousness had worn off. "May I have the pleasure of knowing your name?"

"I am Haven. Haven Cendra," she stated, giving Aaren's hand a small squeeze in the semblance of an informal handshake.

Aaren shut his eyes, thinking. "I know that name. But it couldn't be. The princess of Eringoth, at my bedside?" He opened them again, clear pools of spring water.

"Couch-side, to be exact," she quipped, giving a small smile. "We couldn't really get you to the medical bay in one piece."

Aaren grimaced, and with his other hand ran it along his battered self. His hand eventually rested on the necklace, and he stroked it thoughtfully. "It's funny. I knew you before you even spoke your name."

Haven tiled her head at him, not quite understanding what he meant. She waited for him to elaborate.

"In the Forrest," he continued, almost mesmerized by his hazy memory. "I saw your face and I recognized it without even knowing your name. It was the strangest feeling."

"Have we met before?" Haven queried, thinking back to how he had once met Leonardo as a child.

Aaren shook his head. "I was never able to meet the famed half-human daughter of King Dromo. There were few times that I could leave the…" the prince trailed off, eyes veiling over.

Haven's face clouded with worry. It was a great warning to her that he couldn't even mention his kingdom. Wanting to sustain conversation further while simultaneously avoiding any trauma, Haven pressed on with other matters.

"You have heard of me?" she asked, legitimately curious about what he knew.

Aaren, aware of Haven's obvious deviation of topic, answered with relief. "Of course. You are the lady of our land, after all. Your name has always fascinated me, Haven." He looked at her as if piecing together a legend. "Eringoth. In the ancient tongue it translates as Safe Haven. Does that make you our protector?" his eyes danced with what Haven thought just might be deviousness.

The girl resisted an outright snort. She wanted her first impression to be mildly acceptable. "I'm hardly anyone's protector. Right now I'm just trying to protect myself."

"It is a dark, dark world out there," Aaren agreed softly, glancing out the windows at the pitch black beyond. A moonless night peered in, the blackness threatening to suck the light from the small study area the two shared. Aaren looked down at the hand that held his. He noticed that there were bandages on her palms. Looking up at her, he picked up a strand of bandage and with his eyes asked permission. Haven shrugged and let him unravel the gauze that clung to her hand. She couldn't refuse those eyes.

"It seems that you have a very good reason to protect yourself," Aaren commented, holding her charred hand in his. He peered up at her. "You have been touched by the Goddess."

"What does that even mean?" Haven asked, a bit of exasperation leaking into her tone. People kept saying that, but what were they actually trying to convey to her? "It doesn't appear that the Goddess has touched me very kindly, then," she added, rubbing her other hand on her forehead.

"Your being gives life to flame?" Aaren asked, tracing his thumb on her palm. Blackness rubbed off as he did, but she didn't feel any pain.

Haven nodded. "It's only happened once so far, but I'm still in shock."

"Why, because you carry human blood? You think that limits you?" He was eyeing her now, genuinely interested in her reply.

Haven had never been so forwardly asked about her condition. She was slightly taken aback by his direct approach; she supposed that was the inner ruler emerging- no beating around the bush. "I had never really addressed it as such, but yes. I always thought that because I was human that there was no possible way for me to acquire powers."

Aaren shook his head, a sense of all-knowing tracing his smile. "Humanity is the most unpredictable group of people to ever exist. The power they contain is unlike anything I have ever seen. You must embrace the wildness within you. It will one day become your power."

Haven dropped her gaze, internalizing what Aaren had said. She looked at her hand, encased in his. They were both so similar on the exterior, having five fingers and knuckles and wrists. What churned underneath the surface that made them so different?

"All my life, I've been told otherwise. Humans are weak, it's why they're always in-fighting and dying of disease. I've been led to believe that I have been cursed by the very woman who raised me," Haven felt her bottom lip tremble. There was no way she was going to become emotional in front of this man. It would betray her weakness right there, in front of him.

Aaren shook his head, a frown covering his visage. "Is that what people have told you? They're fools. Humans are much more than the folly they involve themselves in."

Haven felt her lips curve up; Aaren had just indirectly called the most powerful Council in the land foolish.

"You know what," he continued; a thought had struck him. "I believe they are afraid of you. You are something that they cannot predict or control, and that scares them."

"You seem to know a lot about humans and their behavior," Haven commended him, crossing her legs and leaning in closer. "I wish I had known you in my formative years. It would have saved me and my poor family great trouble."

Aaren absent-mindedly ran a hand through his navy hair; it flopped back into his eyes almost immediately. A rainbow of blues glanced in the firelight. "A woman as beautiful as you should never have to endure such troubles."

Haven felt herself reddening in the dim room; she looked away and pretended to wipe an eyelash from her cheek. It was rare when someone other than the knights or her own dear father called her beautiful. "They have made me who I am," she started, continuing on as if the comment hadn't been uttered. "If I wasn't raised on such words, I probably wouldn't have become a knight."

Aaren's quizzical brow betrayed his surprise. "Eringoth's princess. A lady knight?"

It was not well circulated that Haven had obtained the rank of knighthood- those who thought it was a disgrace opted to remain silent for fear of their brothers of other kingdoms to discover it. Haven was mildly amused at Aaren's reaction, for it was purely of surprise and not incredulity.

"The one and only," she stated proudly, drawing herself up a little. "I'm tougher than I look."

Aaren laughed for the first time that evening; a clear laugh, resonant and light. "I never once doubted your stature, not to worry. I knew many small warriors that made the greatest of fighters."

"You mean, the warriors of your homeland?" Haven asked. She most immediately wished she hadn't.

At the mentioning of the West, Aaren's face fell. It became cloaked in shadow; the smile disintegrated. However, this time he did not shy away from the question. "Yes, just like them," he replied softly.

Haven paused for a long time, wondering whether or not she should continue. It might be hours before anyone could catch this man conscious again, and time was of the essence. With discomfort evident in her posture, Haven lowered her voice, following suit. "What happened to them, Aaren?"

A grim smirk was caught in his lips. "I suppose it cannot be avoided. I must speak of my people," he took a moment to compose himself. "Several days ago. My cavalry men and I were on a perimeter ride, ensuring the safety of the boundaries of our small kingdom before we were to set off to the waypoint. It was routine; not many of us were carrying our full arsenal of weaponry. Everything was business as usual until we began to return from the mountains."

Aaren paused then, gathering himself. Haven gave his hand a reassuring squeeze. "Then we saw black smoke, billowing into the sky and choking out the sun. My men and I urged on our steeds, feeling in our hearts that something had gone terribly wrong. We came to the township, and…it was in chaos."

Aaren continued to describe the panic that ensued. Haven saw the images dancing about his head as he spoke, each one consuming him in its own way. Innocent elves lay slain on the ground at the knights' feet, their crumpled bodies expelling blood that blended with the mud stirred up from freshly fallen rain. Huts and houses burned, charred ash filling the air and raining down like soiled snow. For a while, it was uncertain what exactly had been happening. But as the knights pushed through the crowds of fleeing citizens, all became clear.

Aaren shuddered involuntarily, the tremors wracking his entire frame. "There in the heart of the village, were people-creatures. They were indescribable at first glance. Monsters from the black pits of the earth."

Aaren peered up, seeing the questions burning in Haven's eyes. "I shall describe them the best I can," he continued, "I saw six at the town's green but I would not be surprised if more lurked in the shadows of the woods or the castle. The things stood taller than any man or elf that I have ever seen. Their bodies were black, as if charred, and heavily muscled, wearing little to no garments of clothing. Black liquid dripped from their skin and sickeningly long claws. They seemed to once resemble elves, for long ears protruded from their oily scalps," he paused for a moment, perturbed, as if he had just made an important connection for the first time. "Each and every one had blazing red eyes."

Haven stopped for a moment, a thought having struck her. "Leonardo mentioned having seen a man with red eyes in the forest at the rendezvous point."

"I too, met a man in the woods with red eyes. But he was like you and me, not monstrous at all- at least on the surface. He went by the name of Aki," Aaren stated, rubbing the side of his head. "He and a woman helped care for me in my hour of greatest peril."

Haven mulled the appearance of the man over, not sure whether she could peg him as a help or a hindrance. The name was unfamiliar to her, and it wasn't local to Eringothian tongue. He seemed to be linked in with all of the disturbances in recent weeks, but Haven couldn't begin to fathom who or what he was. The existence of a possible third party confused her all the more.

"They had taken me to a thatched hut a little ways south from the remains of my kingdom and tended my wounds. But there was something wrong about the whole scene," Aaren paused, his face twisting in trying to remember the details. "Everything was in a blur, and Aki and the woman disappeared into thin air."

"A mirage?" Haven guessed. Not knowing much about magic herself, the girl took a shot in the dark. "Maybe this Aki person is a spellcaster."

The inference seemed to make sense to Aaren, but there was still something that held him back. "The place didn't feel like magic, though. If it was indeed a fabrication, it was by far the most skilled and complex one I have ever witnessed. The man had incredible power. But he was nether elf nor human. I simply do not understand," his voice suddenly grew tired, as if the heavy thinking was burdening his conscious state. But he forced himself to continue. "And the demons I saw were not civil, as the man who had saved me had been," Aaren continued with a sigh. "They were wild and blind with unheeded rage, lashing out at any man or beast that stood in their way."

"What were they doing in the kingdom? Why in the world were they attacking innocent people?" The princess pressed, the thought of so many lives being lost was becoming increasingly unsettling.

At this question, Aaren's face had become as dark as the calm, low clouds before a storm. "I know exactly who caused this all, and it is with great grief that I say his name. My elder brother, Lord Inness, was both an elf lost in his ways and a great and powerful sorcerer. It was not directly announced, but I am certain that he conjured or summoned those monsters."

"Your own brother?" Haven found herself asking. She had unconsciously put herself in Aaren's shoes, thinking of Kohan and if he would do anything like that to her and her people.

Aaren nodded, his face tight. His eyes began to redden with the hot betrayal that still simmered underneath his calm exterior. "Recognizing my brother's handiwork, I went to the castle to confront him. There was a fear rooted in the darkest corner of my heart, but I couldn't bring myself to realize that fear until it had been played out in front of me." The prince's voice broke as he had approached the words that needed to be spoken next. He cleared his throat and continued on, unnervingly calm. "I found the rest of my family- my father, mother and…" he cleared his throat again. "Little sister, Harmony, in the throne room. My brother was standing over them; the staff in his hand still humming from recent use. I was too late. Inness had claimed the throne of the Western Kingdom for himself."

Aaren's final words echoed throughout the small study room, the weight of his words seemed to bounce off the walls and then seep slowly into the floor. Haven's mouth had fallen open in disbelief; she felt her heart breaking for the prince that lay in front of her. He had turned away again, his form silhouetted in the flickering torches that surrounded them. The elf didn't cry, but the sorrow that streaked across his face was more than enough to unnerve the girl that sat beside him.

"You mean to say that Lord Inness has crowned himself king?" Haven asked, disbelief striking her. Such an irrational act was unheard of in elfin history; even if there had been any attempts to assume the authority of the king, these efforts were always stopped and made in vain.

"That man is no king," Aaren said bitterly, eyes blazing. They flicked to her, and darted away into the shadows again. "He has misused his power and employed his rage to steal something that does not belong to him. He is an imposter."

Haven bit her lip in thought, confused. "You said Inness was the first born. Why is it that he wanted to steal away the crown? Wouldn't he have received it in due time?"

Aaren sighed, shaking his head. "My parents thought my brother to be lost in his ways. He was no leader; locking himself in the tower and performing dark spells. The people feared him and turned to me instead. A little under a year ago, the king and queen announced that the throne would fall to me once my father's time was ended. This, to say the least…unsettled Inness."

The princess was taken aback by this yet again unorthodox gesture to skip the first born's opportunity for the throne. Having never been to the Western kingdom before, she wondered what other oddities occurred that were against the elfin traditions. Living in the North meant that she had been suffocated by such mores. But she didn't find that to be any excuse for the atrocities committed by the eldest son of King Ronan and Queen Talulla.

A surge of wanting swelled within the princess; she wanted desperately to help Aaren in his plight. For the citizens of the West and for the lost prince that lay before her. All of this time Haven had thought that the lot she had been given was unfair and harsh. A daughter of two worlds but belonging to neither. Now, she witnessed an elf who had lost everything; his family, his people, his future kingship. She felt that no one in this beautiful land should have to suffer such a great loss.

"Aaren. If there is anything the Kingdom of Eringoth can do for you, please. Let me know." She took his hand in both of hers. "And if there is anything I can do for you, give the summons and I will be there. I may not have much swing with the Council, but I am the daughter to the King. I can definitely be of assistance to you."

A slight smile crossed Aaren's face. "Just having someone here to converse with is all I need right now. I fear I may have gone mad if I was left alone with my thoughts. Thank you, Haven."

The princess felt herself reddening; she was thankful for the dim lighting situation of the study. She decided to press on, not dwelling on the prince's gratitude. "What are you going to do?"

Aaren forced an empty laugh. "The first step would be concentrating on my recovery. I can't reclaim a kingdom if it is hard for me to even walk."

"So you're going back?" Haven asked, intrigued. A plan began to formulate inside her head.

"It is my duty. By the declaration of my father, I am the rightful heir of the Western throne. There are people back there who need my guidance. And I am the only one who can stand up to my brother," Aaren professed, his jaw tightening. Determination flickered in his eyes. "There was a time when I had almost forgotten that. It will not happen again."

Just as Aaren's eyes had begun to glow with an inner strength that surprised Haven, a rolling of thunder rocked the exterior of the castle. The two turned to the windows, curtains draped to the side, to observe the coming nightly storm. The grounds beyond flickered in a lightning strike; the objects Haven knew to be flowers and vegetation carried the silhouettes of distorted creatures writing in agony. The night brought on terrible new form to the world outside. The spattering of rain on the windows made Haven grateful that she and Leonardo recovered the prince when they did.

Haven turned back to converse with Aaren, but his eyes were still fixed on the windows. His complexion had fallen pale once more and shock had etched itself into his face. Bewildered, Haven turned to follow his gaze back to the outside.

There, where a moment before there had been nothing but castle grounds, framed by the glass, stood a dark figure. His form was right against the window, peering in on the warm study room. Haven's heart jumped into her throat. Immediately she leapt from her seat, putting herself between the window and the injured prince. In the dim gleamed two burning eyes, bright as small red suns.

Realization stuck Haven like a bolt of lightning; she shied away from the intense gaze as her mind scrambled to make a plan. Exasperated by not having any weapons on her, Haven crouched and tore off the bandages on her hands, forcing her eyes on the form in the window. She tried not to let the sling at her shoulder impede her. "I know who you are," she murmured dangerously.

"Do you believe that I'm intimidated by you, Haven Cendra?" A low, smug voice rung out in her mind; Aaren's hands flew to his temples, evidently he could hear the sound too.

"What do you want, Aki?" Aaren shouted, his voice husky after only muttering for so long. Haven stepped back, surprised that the prince had addressed him directly.

"Remember. Your time is running out with every breath you breathe. Every day is a day closer to your demise." The figure declared, his voice striking inside of Haven's mind, the words ricocheting around in her head.

Lightning flickered again, and the figure vanished from sight. Haven approached the window cautiously, every step she made with utter care. Upon the next jolt of thunder and the flash coming soon after, Haven felt a blast of misty air and shattering glass. She stumbled back. Rain sprayed on her cheeks and she covered her eyes against the spattering. Torches and candles in the room were smeared out by the harsh wind and the room was pitched into darkness. Light now streamed from the exterior, where the nighttime colors coursed in with greys and blues, striking into the black castle.

Haven tripped backwards, calling out to the prince. "Aaren, are you okay?"

"Just fine, milady," Aaren replied. From where his voice was traveling it seemed that the man was attempting to rise from his resting place.

Cold fear was trickling into Haven's veins. What was happening? What did Aki mean, that Aaren's time was running out? With the increasing fear came shortened breaths. She tried to stop and think, what to do first.

Find a light source. Locate the intruder.

Haven thought first of stumbling around in the dark in search of matches and a candle. She shook her head. That would take too much time. This man had to be located. The princess had a thought. She flexed her hands, palms facing upward. On her skin, smoldering hot but not harming the flesh, simmered small embers, glowing bright in the night. Orange light curled around the small chunks of heat, an occasional spark leaping up at her. A light smoke curled into her nose. *If only there was a way I could make these brighter.*

"I see you've discovered your gift, Haven Cendra."

Haven whirled around, black hair billowing, to face Aki. In one swift movement, she turned on the balls of her feet and let her hands flare as brightly as her emotions did. Surprise in her heart led the flames at her palms to catch, and by the time she stood squarely with the man her hands were containing small golden flames. Aki had been standing there the whole time, studying her; the night had been his disguise. The new firelight distorted the smirk on his face into a monstrous grin.

"By the power vested in me as the princess of this land, I demand you to state your business here," Haven ordered, eyes wide but voice steady.

Aki grinned all the more so that his teeth flashed white. "You don't even understand how to use it, do you? Poor girl. I may have been a little amused by you if you did."

In the dim light of the room, Aaren had managed to find a crutch left for him by the Healers and was standing on his own. Aki made a move to start walking toward the prince, but Haven stepped in his path.

"What are you doing here? Who are you?" Haven fired, holding her palms out so that the flames could breathe. They flickered and trembled as she did, but she held her ground.

Aki's lip curled up in minor annoyance. The cloak about him billowed menacingly, blackening out his form so that just his pale face could be seen. "Out of my way, princess. I'd hate to have to harm such an interesting human specimen."

"How do you know about me?" Haven asked, genuinely curious but buying time as well. She hoped that attendants- anyone- would come shortly, noticing that something was wrong.

"I know many things," Aki started enigmatically, stepping toward Haven slowly. "I am a man of the mind. And I know that there are forces at work in this land that have broken the balance of Nature. The Goddess is not pleased."

"What are you, some sort of monk?" Haven snipped, flexing her hands. The flames in them jumped expectantly. She felt herself becoming lightheaded for some reason, her breathing was quick and short.

Aki openly laughed, a clear and terrible sound, as if the only laughter he had ever experienced was tinged with bitterness. "I am anything but a monk, you poor soul. But that is not for you to discover. This is about the prince, and what he must do," The man's blood red eyes burned as he eyed Haven down. A feral glimmer slipped into them that made her cringe beneath him. "So get out of my way."

Haven made no motion, and said nothing that indicated her surrender. There was something unsettling about this man, and Haven wasn't about to let him get any closer to the damaged prince. She wanted answers, and if he wasn't going to give them to her, he was going to have to face her.

The man raised an eyebrow when Haven fell as still as a statue. "Have it your way, then."

Aki raised his arm, as if to strike the girl from his path. Haven reacted immediately by swiping a hand in front of her face, making contact with the wrist meant to attack her. A trail of sparks flew in the arch of her gesture, and upon the collision, flames leapt out in all directions. The room was temporarily lit with a spider web of light, highlighting the shock on everyone's face in the room.

Haven had little time to marvel at her new power, however, because it appeared that Aki was done with her shenanigans. She could sense the muscles tensing in his body as he prepared to attack. The only thing that kept Haven from running was the small flame of courage lit in her chest, reflected literally in the flames at her hands. Aki lunged forward with lightning speed, wrapping a hand around the wrist that had collided with him. Haven twisted under his arm, avoiding the blow from his other hand. She flexed her ensnared hand and a burst of flame, coupled with his contorted arm, forced Aki to let her go.

The opponents sprung back and circled one another slowly. Thunder accented the noiseless scene and white light splashed over the room, temporarily washing out their faces. After the flash, Haven heard a dark chuckle, chilling her down to her bones. "Nice footwork, little girl. It seems as though you have learned a thing or two from the king's pets."

Haven gritted her teeth and ignored the taunting, knowing a biting remark would only goad him on. She took the opportunity to search for Aaren, who had fallen silent during the confrontation. The couch was empty and the only movement she could detect was the billowing of the hospital sheets as they shied away from the blustering wind. Silently Haven hoped that he was out somewhere looking for help. She eyed Aki as he crouched in an almost savage manner, his eyes burning in the night. Haven knew she wasn't strong in hand-to-hand combat, but was aware at the same time that she had to give the illusion that she did.

Aki waited for Haven to make the first move. The princess curled her fingers around the flames that leapt from her palms and jumped forward. She focused on her energy and thought of how she could launch her power into projectiles. Almost as immediately as she conceived the thought, embers and hot fire shot across the room. The mysterious man's eyes glinted with amusement; he hurdled to the side, easily dodging the attack. He rebounded on one hand and landed upright again, unfazed. The flames splintered as they hit the frame of the open window behind Aki. Small fires began to take root on the sills and nearby carpet.

The being didn't pause for a moment. This time, he lunged forward to Haven, who stumbled backwards, surprised at his speed. He had to be at least as fast as a trained elf, but like others had said before, there was something distinctly un-elfin about the way he moved. Haven was taken aback when she blinked and Aki was immediately in her air space. In one swift motion, he grabbed her wrist and captured the fire that inhabited it, spinning the golden glow in his own fingers with incredible dexterity. Haven felt a great strength leave her body when the flames were snatched from her.

Aki stared at the flame for a moment, his hand caressing the intangible form of fire. "Fire is not suited for the weak of heart, princess. You ought to reconsider brandishing it so foolishly."

And before Haven could even muster a rebuttal, Aki launched an orb of fire from his palm. It hurtled toward Haven, rolling and increasing in size until it was akin to that of a cannon ball. Biting her lip and acknowledging that she could not take the blow head-on, Haven dove as the projectile sailed forth. The smell of singed hair instantly filled the room and the girl crashed to the floor. Her wounded shoulder hit the ground first; she resisted the urge to shriek in pain.

There was no time to react to physical unpleasantness. The ball of fire had crashed into a bookshelf behind her. The massive shelf, at least fifteen feet high, had a blackened hole where impact was made; flaming books rained down on the princess, burning pages floating through the air as fallen angels. Smoke filled the room and further masked the man in black. Then: the sickening snap of wood. Books began to rain down upon her; tomes of ancient law codes and histories of elfin war toppled onto her fallen form.

Haven knew she had to move, and fast. Her body screamed with the drain from using her new power, but the girl managed to pull herself up and scramble away from the shelf as it began to topple down. She sighted Aki from the corner of her eye; he looked on with mild interest, but made no further move to attack her. Pulling herself out of the way just in time, the bookshelf crashed on to a study table, crushing the piece of furniture and simultaneously splitting in half.

On her hands and knees and catching her breath, Haven saw a burst of cold blue light. There was a crack, and Aki toppled to the ground as well, a grunt of surprise leaving his lips when he hit the floor. The air immediately dropped a few degrees, and the cold form of ice bloomed from the spot where Aki lay. Haven whipped around to find Aaren standing there, hands balled into fists and as white as snow. He exhaled a deep breath, frost billowing from his mouth. The princess lay there in shock, staring up at Aaren. He stood on his own, bare feet planted firmly in place. Where his toes touched the carpet, there was a twinkling of freshly produced frost.

Aaren's eyes glinted a cold blue in the darkness. His breath came in small bursts, but his face remained calm. As soon as he had delivered the arctic blast, he dropped his stance and dragged himself to where Haven was.

Haven looked up at him, eyes wide. "You carry the Goddess's gift?"

Aaren grimaced modestly, his body stiff with pain. "One might assume that."

The princess wanted to say more but motion caught the corner of her eye. Aki moved about the edge of the study, remaining in the shadow. His black garb was dappled with shavings of ice, but he didn't seem to notice.

"I'm impressed, Aaren," he began. The demonic light had receded from his face, but Haven could still see it churning beneath his molten eyes. "With that spirit, you may have a chance."

Grabbing each other for support, Haven and Aaren struggled to their feet. Their eyes darted around warily, attempting to locate the intruder who had vanished into the shadows once more.

"Whatever business you have with me, Aki, leave Haven out of this. She is not your foe." Aaren called out. The silence neither confirmed nor denied the understanding of the man in black.

"What does he want?" Haven hissed, hoping the rain and wind would hide her voice.

Aaren braced himself, standing on his own. He shook his head. "When we met before, I couldn't-"

"My wish is to speak with the prince, alone. I am the keeper of information that I know he would like to be privy to." Aki cut in, disembodied voice slicing through the dark and making the two flinch.

Haven leaned into the prince, shuttering. "Aaren, he may have helped you, but no one can be sure of his intentions. He might be trying to manipulate you for his own purposes."

Aaren nodded, and the two spread out. Haven reached for several surgical tools by the couch while Aaren spoke out: "Whatever you need to say can be spoken to the both of us."

Haven could almost hear the grin in Aki's voice. "Sorry, wrong answer. You know how humans can talk."

A yelp escaped Haven's lips when needle-like daggers struck out from the darkness, heading straight for her. She brought up her hands, feeling the heat pulsing from them melt the tiny missiles. Others struck her legs as she danced around the projectiles, sending ribbons of pain through her muscles. More were deflected from an icy blast sent from Aaren's direction. He slumped with the effort, watching with wide eyes as Aki emerged again.

He seemed to rise from the shadows, running full-tilt at the princess of Eringoth. She stumbled back in attempt to dodge a fresh wave of needles, landing flat on her back with a grunt.

Aaren lifted his hands into the air, summoning recently frozen tomes from the ground. They swirled about his body, gathering speed until the prince lunged forward, sending his new weapons hurtling at Aki. The intruder deftly dodged, vaulting and pitching around them. Iced- over books of all sizes slammed into the wall behind Aki, sending tremors through the room. An encyclopedia struck him in the temple, throwing discord into his dance.

Haven took the opportunity to gather herself, brandishing the few sharp medical tools she had picked up. Desperation closed her throat shut- she wasn't backing down, and that made the man in black all the more eager to stop her. Once in the clear of the book barrage, Aki hurtled forward with a dark grin, hands revealing incredibly sharp fingernails from within his cloak. His sights were set on Haven.

Their eyes met- the contact sent tendrils of fear pulsing through her. Compartmentalizing her emotions was necessary to survive; Haven forced them deep down and focused on the raw physical action in front of her. The lady knight remembered her training and tensed her body, analyzing her opponent's movements.

In moments Aki had crossed the room and entered Haven's weapon radius. She pitched a small scalpel at his middle; the missile glinted in the small fires that speckled the room. It was an easy dodge for her opponent, but it slowed him down just so Haven could roll opposite him.

Your defiance growing tiring rather fast, princess. I think I may have to end this sooner than you would like, Aki's voice cooed in her head. She bit down the urge to say something back- it was all a distraction.

You are going to wish you never stood up to me, he grinned, baring teeth that flashed in the dark.

And with that he lunged, and the two fell into a deadly dance. Aki took the offensive, driving Haven back toward the wall. Aaren continued to assist from a distance, sending icy assailants o toward Aki. He held up well against the two, however, and that meant he was using time to drain them both. Haven dodged lunges and kicks that became more ferocious with time. On one hand, she was pleased that her training could frustrate such a dangerous foe, but this drove more power and intention into his every step. He was done with the games.

Haven melted another medical tool-she was realizing the less she thought about the magic how easily it came to her- and threw it into an opening in Aki's defenses. His cloak tore with a burning hiss and for a moment, his countenance flared with a combination of amusement and rage.

Aki jumped back out of range. *It's no wonder they had your mother killed,* His grin contorted when he spotted the mortification on Haven's face.

She felt the scalpels loosen in her grip, fighting stance slowing. Her brain screamed to keep her guard up, but something deep inside shut down her will to move.

From across the room, Aaren noticed her slackening posture. "Haven! What is going on?" He had collapsed from the use of his magic and no longer had the strength to stand.

Aki cocked his head back in triumph. He knew a nerve had been hit. *That's right. We both know what really happened all those years ago. But no one would believe you, even if you told the truth. They would only laugh. What a silly little human.*

"How do you…" Haven trailed off, mind racing the speed of sound. Her mother's face melted into view, her soft face blurred by the age of the memory.

In a flash, Aki was in her face again, one hand on the wrist that held her weapons and the other cupped skillfully around her neck.

"I am everywhere. I see everything. And how I know will no longer be a concern of yours." He whispered, soft and sharp into her ear.

Haven felt disconnected from her body, all nerves mute. She could only focus on the man's voice, and the words that her soul absorbed like a dark poison. Someone else knew. She looked into Aki's scorching eyes one final time and truly believed the secret would die with her.

Time and noise evaporated from the scene, and Haven braced for a fatal blow.

"Not so fast, stranger. I'm afraid I can't let you kill my princess." a voice rung out.

An explosion of noise rocked the study, and to everyone's surprise, an army of crows descended upon the intruder, soaring in from the broken window. They flocked about his face and pecked at exposed skin, driving Aki back.

Everyone whipped around to find Leonardo at the entrance of the study, hands shoved forward. His eyes were light with determination. Feathers swirled about the space in a small cyclone; Haven, though still numb, took the opportunity to scramble out of danger.

Aaren turned to face the newest member on the scene, bewildered. The frosty aura surrounding him flickered with curiosity.

Leonardo jumped forward, shouting above his winged friends. "Prince Aaren, it's been a while. But this is no time to catch up. It seems that we have a debacle on our hands." He pressed into the room. Aaren nodded, looking slightly confused but embracing the presence of a new ally.

Leonardo flicked his wrist and the crows ascended. Where Aki had been, there was empty space. Gathering Haven from the floor, he paled at her bewildered expression. "What happened, princess? I'm glad I came back when I did. Who was that man?"

All Haven could do was shake her head and let herself be taken in by her friend. The rush from the battle began to subside, and for the first time she felt shooting pain in her hands and shoulder. She didn't dare to check their condition. All she could think about was her mother.

Her musings, however, were interrupted by shouting from outside the study. The doorway began to illuminate with the approaching of torches.

From the other side of the room Aki had risen and stood like a stone, eerie and motionless, watching them. "It's a pity I can't stay and chat longer. We can thank the little princess for that." He turned to Haven with a smirk.

Haven recovered her faculties enough to snort. Her emerald eyes burned. "I don't know what you are, but you can hold me to it that I'm going to find out. Sorry for the inconvenience."

Aki clicked his tongue at her. "How like your mother you are." His eyes gleamed with the greatest knowing. "Curiosity could get you killed one day." Breath caught in her throat, silencing her. Leonardo regarded her with a wary eye.

Aki turned to Aaren, but made no move to approach him. "Remember what I told you, Western Prince. I know we will meet again." Aki warned quietly. An instant of knowing passed between the two men, and Aaren's face fell dark.

Immediately after, the study flooded with several pages and servants, led by Sir Gideon and followed closely by Sir Ailill and two other knights. They were dressed in evening garb- from the looks of it, they had been interrupted at dinner. Upon seeing the condition of the study, a wreck of burning embers and ice, Gideon and Ailill both drew their weapons.

"Captain!" Haven struggled to keep her voice strong, incredibly relieved that help had finally arrived. She pointed in the direction of the open window, to where Aki had crouched yet again. "An intruder has entered the castle."

Gideon stepped forth cautiously, his eyes glinting dangerously from under his shaggy brown hair. He assessed the damage of the room in a quick glance, then spoke with authority to

Aki. "State your business here. Your unlawful entry is a crime against the Crown. Speak and we may reduce your punishment."

Aki let his lips spread into another amused smirk; it was the only detectable movement in his form. Yet another streak of lightning flashed outside, blinding all in the room. When the darkness returned, Aki was gone. The men in the doorway were about to come rushing in, but a voice filtered into everyone's head and forced all to stop.

"I owe no allegiance to any business. Yet there is no business that is not mine. Hurry onward, little prince. Do not forget what I have told you."

Haven clutched at her head, hating that somehow Aki could get inside. Gideon wasted not a second in sending people to search the room and put out the small fires that had sprung up. He summoned Ailill and the other knights, drawing them close and whispering intensely in their midst. The knights rushed out; Ailill, giving a nod to Haven as he left.

Gideon approached the prince and princess, bowing as he neared and then kneeling beside them. "A search party is being assembled as we speak. That man is going to be contained and questioned for the heinous act committed here. Are you two all right?" By the end the concern in his voice had outweighed the authority.

"You are not going to find him," Aaren murmured, looking out the opened window. Servants were assessing the damage and peering out into the storm. "He will be long out of our reach before the party is assembled."

"We have to try," Haven insisted, looking at Gideon. Her own heart spoke the next words, desperation tinting her voice. "We need answers."

Gideon nodded. "And you both need medical attention. This fight is long from over, and our kingdom needs both of you in good condition. I'll send for the Healers and I'll come down with a progress report later. Leonardo, look after them." He patted Haven on the shoulder as he rose. "I see that gift of yours has come in handy, lass. Just be careful. A great power flows in you."

Gideon left Haven, Aaren and Leonardo to themselves as he questioned the pages for any clues found on the premises. They were lost in their own thoughts; looking at each other, equally perplexed.

"Whatever Aki meant, Aaren, I want to help. I'll slow the clock." Haven said at last, opting to conceal the private conversation she had with Aki. Whatever that man had come for had to do with the immediate present, and Aaren's kingdom. Her mother would have to wait.

Leonardo, not fully aware of what had happened, but wanting to support the navy-haired elf, nodded in agreement. The three of them sat in the ruined room, rubble strewing the floor and papers fluttering through the air. The rain continued to trickle outside, a soft backdrop to their reverie.

Aaren said nothing; he was in a world that none but he could enter. A shadow had been pulled across his brow ever since Aki had left the scene. He mulled over all that the man had said and stroked his necklace, entranced with a loathing that began to suffocate his heart.

Nine
AAREN

THE DAYS PASSED BY; storms came and went. As Aaren had predicted, the search party assembled by the Captain of the Guard had recovered no trace of the intruder. If there had been any evidence or hint as to where Aki had fled, the traces were washed away by the storm from that evening. More guards were posted at the palace entrances that usual, and an air of paranoia began to filter through the halls. With the assassination attempt on the prince and now with a violent break-in, the inhabitants of the castle were on edge.

Word spread quickly through the halls that Haven had recovered a Western Prince in the Royal Forrest. Amongst these whispers were questions as to why Haven had been alone in the woods with a knight in the first place. As with anything that surrounded the princess, rumor had gotten out of hand. From the bedside telling of maidens and Healers in his comfortable bedchambers, Aaren heard all manner of slandering accusations made about Princess Haven. He did not take these comments at face value by any means. Aaren listened acutely when the servants believed him to be asleep in recovery.

In conjunction with the mentioning of Haven's name came the title of Sir Leonardo, from the East. The name was a familiar one to Aaren, as if he were the protagonist from a story told to him long ago as a child. It was known in the castle that he spent a lot of time with the princess upon his arrival from the East. With the guesswork he made, Aaren assumed that Leonardo was the man he had seen in the forest and later in the study room. He wondered if he belonged to the battalion of knights that the West intended to rendezvous with in the woods.

Aaren received a number of infrequent but extended visits from the princess. On occasion, Sir Leonardo would join her; Aaren became reacquainted with his childhood friend. The more he talked with the knight the greater his memory was stirred, and before long the two were sharing stories of simpler times and gathering information on old acquaintances.

On the other hand, Haven was rather concerned about his well-being, which charmed and amused the prince. Even though his condition had been much more severe, he healed at a faster rate. Haven's human blood disadvantaged her; he could see the envy glinting in her eyes with every bandage removed from his body. She was finally allowed to remove the cast that held her wounded shoulder, but it was still tender and Aaren could tell that it irked her.

The first few visits that the princess made were rather stiff ones; after the scuffle in the lounge it was clear that Haven wanted to talk, but she wasn't quite sure about what. It was hard for Aaren to make himself talk to anyone at all; most days he wanted to be alone with his thoughts. At first he forced himself to wear a presentable countenance, all the while grieving inwardly. But he found that as he continued to talk to Haven that he could forget for a while about his troubles. Something about her charmed him; it took him a while to realize that it was her sincerity and honesty that drew him out from his own shields.

After re-hashing what had occurred in the study several times, the two managed to branch out to other matters. Aaren found himself able to speak of his homeland more freely, and he could tell that it was the same for her. When Aaren was well enough to walk, they would stroll in the gardens that surrounded the castle or Haven would give tours of different sections of the palace. It felt good to move about and embrace the warm sun. It was a particularly beautiful time of year in the North, as the gardens were in bloom and the castle, bustling. It was another world, compared to the small settlement that was the Western Kingdom. Aaren found himself gaping at the history that laid itself out before him; while the West was only a few generations old, the North had been around for much, much longer.

There was one particular occasion that, after one such tour, the two were sharing mid-morning tea. The sitting room in which they rested held other groups of elves, all chatting quietly and enjoying the warm sun that bathed all surfaces in yellow light. Occasionally, other elves would peer over at the Eringothian royals and turn back to whisper amongst themselves.

Aaren had rested his elbows on the table and cradled a warm cup of lemon tea in his hands. The fingers that held the delicate ceramic cup were riddled with cuts that were sealed over with fresh scar tissue. Little purple slashes with new pink skin surrounding it seemed to grow darker against the white cup. Aaren would smile at a comment made by the woman across from him; occasionally he could taste the iron of blood in his mouth from a cracked lip. Despite these minor frailties that exposed hardship undergone, the prince's pallor had returned to a healthy glow. Although his skin was naturally lighter than any other Northern and certainly Eastern elf, a blush now accented his cheeks where before there was naught but a thin grey.

He smiled at his companion as she tried to speak. Her own complexion had been turning ruddier by the second- another human trait passed on by her mother- as she attempted to formulate a question that had been on her mind for some time now. Aaren liked the expressive quality of her features; it was like watching a constantly changing painting. The way she would bite her lip while she was thinking, or how she would unconsciously twirl her hair entertained the prince. He watched her hands as she did so now; delicate white threading in and out of her coal black hair. Sometimes her hand could get caught in a knot and she would be in a fluster to untangle herself. Aaren attempted to hide a grin whenever such a thing would happen; he was rarely successful.

"You. You have powers like me." Haven said at last, looking Aaren in the eye. Two emeralds locked in his attention from across the table.

Aaren took a sip from his drink, eyeing her thoughtfully. "Indeed. This is a known fact." He deliberately avoided finishing the thought for her; he wanted to see what she had to say.

Haven looked down and through the scone on her plate, ordering her words. Sometimes they were well thought out and others not, but Haven was almost always speaking her mind.

"Well, I had been wondering recently…how you control it so well," Haven began again, refusing to look up from her scone. A hand still toyed with a lock of hair.

Since the attack in the study, Aaren had demonstrated once or twice on a small scale what he could accomplish with his powers. With a single touch he had turned a hot towel for relaxing his muscles into an icy, prickly rock. In another instance, he had waved his hand over a window that held the morning dew. The drops crystallized and webbed onto the glass, little frozen jewels, as Haven gasped in wonder.

Aaren remained silent, watching Haven but not giving her any help. He waited for her to continue.

"I talked to some of the mages in the village," Haven started with a sigh. "In the large willow trees. Most of them turned me away, saying a human was never meant to tamper with magic. The others who were less harsh but no more receptive still turned me out, but gave me a few books, telling me to read and learn more. But half of them are in the ancient tongue, of which I have very little understanding." She crinkled her nose in frustration, now giving the blueberry scone an uncomfortable glare.

"And it is always better to learn by doing than by reading," Aaren added, privately thinking it ridiculous that she was given books. Magic, like many other things, was interactive. There was more to powers than just reading about and understanding it textually.

"I always hated reading," Haven muttered, almost unconsciously. "I respect scholars what they do and everything," she added quickly, not wanting to sound uncouth. "I just can't handle much heavy reading. I more admire the sword arts and stratagems of battle."

"As I have noticed," Aaren quipped with a slight grin. Haven had gone into passions before about the arts of battle and being physically fit. He had come into the habit of not stopping her, and letting her go until she caught herself.

Haven puffed out her lower lip, catching his joke. "Then you understand my predicament."

"So what you really need is a mentor," Aaren finished for her, knowing the direction in which her query was headed.

Haven met his eyes for a moment. They were intense and sincere. Without saying anything at all Aaren understood how important this had become to her. "I need to control this," she said, looking at her hands and closing them into fists. She had gloved them once more, to conceal her blackened skin.

Aaren sipped again from his tea. "What in your mind has convinced you that I would help you?"

Haven would have taken offense, but the intonation of Aaren's voice put her at ease. She lifted an eyebrow at him. "You may owe me a favor for something."

Aaren chuckled into his cup. "I am indeed grateful for that. I don't think I have thanked you enough for recovering me from the wilderness."

"You can thank me even further by teaching me the ways of the magical arts," Haven added, tilting her head to the side. She added three lumps of sugar to her tea; Aaren wondered how one could deal with such sweetness, and if it was perhaps a human tendency.

Aaren pretended to contemplate on the issue, as if it was a difficult decision. "If you listen to every word I say, and refrain from lighting your mentor ablaze when things get tough," he said at last. "I understand you become easily frustrated."

To this, Haven laughed out loud. A few heads turned in her direction, but she didn't seem to notice. "No fires of revenge, I promise."

"It's a deal, then." Aaren reached his hand across the table for Haven to shake. She took it with a grin, and the pact was sealed.

"When do we start?" She asked eagerly, moving her chair closer to the table. The light of excitement danced in her eyes. "I can make time this afternoon."

Aaren waggled his finger at her. "I would advise speaking with the king first. You wanted to have a word with him, did you not?"

The princess's eyes lit up. "Yes, yes. That does need to be taken care of. I really do hope he understands."

For the past couple days, as the team that was to reclaim the West was being assembled, Haven had been meaning to lobby her father for a position on the journey. Sir Leonardo had already been elected to go on the quest, as both his scholarly and knightly training were sure to come in handy. It was also a given that Aaren was to join them, as he had some personal business to attend to in conjunction with reclaiming his kingdom. As the rightful ruler of the West, he had played an integral part in choosing who would accompany him. Aaren had already put in a good word for the princess, but he gathered it would take more than that to let the king's only daughter go on such a dangerous quest.

Aaren nodded silently, mulling it over. "As do I. So until you receive an answer, your training comes second. If you are allowed on the force, we will have ample time to practice learning your skills."

Haven nibbled at her scone, new resolve forming in her eyes. She put it down a moment later, thinking, and stood. "Aaren, I believe I am going to address this with my father presently. The sooner I have his confirmation, the quicker the rest of this will fall into place."

"I understand. I wish you the very best, Haven. I will be in my quarters later this afternoon if you want to relay the results to me." Aaren stated, remaining seated but patting Haven on the arm as she gathered herself in preparation to leave.

A smile spread across her face at the invitation. "That sounds wonderful."

And before anything else could be said, Haven strode from the room. Aaren watched her leave, grinning at the white blouse she wore- obviously her elder brother's- and the pants she had rolled up to the knees. A part of him wondered if she was going to change before presenting herself to the king of Eringoth.

Aaren remained at the table, spreading butter onto a scone as he mused. He earnestly hoped that Haven could accompany him and his men. A fascination had taken root for this half-human woman, and he wanted her to be able to realize her full talents. More than that- he wanted to know her better.

The prince was left alone in the tea room with his thoughts.

Ten

HAVEN

HAVEN JOGGED- NEARLY RAN- to the throne room, where she knew her father would be spending his time. For a certain number of hours in the week, King Dromo resided in the Hall of Kings with the doors opened wide. At this time, citizens from the palace or from the town could enter and ask advice of or express worries to the king. It was a new policy Dromo had enacted, and for the past several years it had been immensely successful. The king had been able to better access the thoughts of the people, and consequently gauge what codes should and should not be passed.

The princess came to the throne room, her heart beating quickly even when her pace had slowed. There was a decent amount of citizens in line today; they trailed out the entrance of the room and down the hall. Haven stopped for a moment, considering whether or not she wanted to run into the throne room and request a private audience with her father. She looked on at the people who stood in line- weavers, scholars, knights, maids, merchants and tradesmen, even some children. Something inside Haven refused to cut in front of all of these patient people.

By the time she had reached the end of the line, she was already regretting her decision. Haven knew she was bound to get impatient rather quickly. She found herself waiting behind one such of the small children, a young elf boy. His waxy hair seemed to be made of light feathers and his cherub face turned, peering into Haven's.

The boy stared for a while, taking in Haven's dark hair and short stature. Wide eyes, free from a lifetime of predispositions and assumptions met with Haven's own green ones.

"You're beautiful," he gasped, reaching a hand up.

Haven knelt to the boy's level, cheeks reddening. "Why thank you, young sir," she smiled. The child's small hand found her mass of black hair; he stroked it with disbelief.

"How does it get this dark?" He asked, using two hands now. "Is it some type of spell?"

Haven patted the top of the boy's head. "My mother gave me this color. It was hers, too."

The child's eyes grew big. It seemed he was trying to imagine what it was like to have a mother with black hair. The concept of it not being entirely elfin was beyond him. "She must be just as beautiful."

Haven smiled, forcing the thought of Aki and her mother out of her mind. She tried not to wonder how he knew what he knew as the two continued to stroke each other's hair.

The line continued to dwindle as the day went on, and Haven found herself pondering on what to pack for the journey ahead. Her favorite sword, the best saddle, riding clothes, salves and ointments, quiver and bow. Haven knew she would have to pack quickly, Aaren and Leonardo both mentioned they might set out as early as the next day. The list continued to grow as she sat and waited. By the time lunch had rolled around, most of everyone had seen the king.

Soon enough Haven was able to enter the Hall of Kings. The ceiling stretched up high, in a cathedral-like manner, with arches meeting in the center of the roof with several elegant chandeliers hanging down. More high and thin windows lined each side of the hall, stained glass streaking the floors with glues, greens and golds. A single red carpet covered the marble and stretched down the center of the room- the rest of which was empty save for decorative plants and several palace guards.

Haven approached the back of the room to the Seat of Mighty Kings. It was several steps higher than the average elf stood, comprised of a series of oak roots that seemed to grow right out of the stone. The roots laced themselves together to form a beautiful throne; leaves sprouted at the top of the chair and flowers wreathed the bottom. Behind the throne was another wall comprised largely of glass that overlooked the grounds of the castle, which were just starting to come into bloom. Topiary gardens were beginning to receive splashes of red and yellow from blooming flowers, and the willows that dotted the landscape swayed in the spring breeze.

And finally on the throne itself, sat venerable King Dromo. He wore his court finery, which was a cotton robe and a red sash about his waist. The crown of thorns wreathed about his head seemed to carry its own glow. His red Enthima crystal glinted in the afternoon sunlight.

Haven came to her father in a bow, realizing that she probably should have changed clothes. Hair fell on either side of her face as she lowered her head; she cringed inwardly when she saw all the knots that the small child had left behind.

"Rise, my daughter." Dromo ordered. His voice sounded weary from a day of counseling, but it still echoed throughout the hall with great authority.

Haven straightened and took in her father. The day had been long for him; in addition to his open door policy he had been meeting with the Council of Elders, among other things. In light of recent troubles in the castle, the king had many things on his mind.

"My lord, I had been meaning to speak with you for some time now," Haven started.

When she had paused to muster up the thoughts in her mind, Dromo stepped in. "And I, you, my sweet Haven. I had been doing some research, and I discovered the nature of the man who has intruded our castle."

Haven deflated, exasperated after all the waiting. But a different side flared up at the mentioning of the intrusion; she bit her tongue and held back the array of emotions that came in tow.

She folded her hands behind her back and paused for Dromo to elaborate.

"Our friend who goes by the name of Aki is a distant cousin of the elves, belonging to a race of peoples many of us believed to be completely died out," Dromo laced his hands together, elbows resting on either arm of the throne. "They were last known to reside in the upper most region of the Petoac Mountains, where the harsh winter environment led to their isolation. A tribal people, steeped in magic and their own psychic powers, were thought to have been erased from the earth- we haven't seen one for nearly three generations."

"Who are they?" Haven asked, silently wondering if once-scholar Leonardo had any idea who these people were. She was unaware that such a people existed, and wondered if all were as lethal as Aki.

"They were-are- known as the Auranon. Legend has it the Auranon have blood red eyes because they sold their souls to demons in exchange for their incredible powers. They are the ultimate sorcerers, masters of crafting illusions, and have the uncanny capacity to dissolve their own presence-or aura- making them some of the stealthiest individuals in all of Eringoth." Dromo stated, rubbing a temple. Evidently he himself was still internalizing this new and rather immediate threat.

"What is an Auranon doing all the way out here, then? It sounds like this Aki was definitely out of his element. What does he want?" Haven thought back to the encounter, how everything made so much sense now- his voice in everyone's head, the covertness, his dynamic movements.

"I have the feeling that only Prince Aaren knows the answer to that, and I believe even he doesn't know that full truth about this creature," Dromo speculated. "But as I understand it, there is something that Aki wants. I have a feeling that we will be seeing him again in the future. I am uncertain of his personal aims, but if it involves jeopardizing my people, my tolerance for him will wear quite thin."

"I barely have any left," Haven interjected, clenching her fists. "Almost crushing me with a bookcase hasn't exactly put me on good terms with him, no matter his motives."

Dromo sighed, a paternal gleam- worry blended with a sprinkling of pride- entering his silver eyes. "I know I had mentioned this previously, but I am pleased with the manner in which you dealt with the intrusion. Prince Aaren may have been wounded further if you weren't there to stop Aki. You did your kingdom a great service."

It was Haven's turn to sigh. "Other than destroying half of the study, that is. I heard the scholars were in a bit of an uproar about that."

Dromo smiled. "The scholars will be in an uproar over just about anything. It's best just to let them run their course. Most of the books have been salvaged."

"Because the search for Aki has proved fruitless, what are we going to do next?" Haven asked. "Will the investigation extend beyond the palace grounds?" If anything, she wanted something to go on regarding Aki's location. Granted, it wasn't the greatest idea, but she needed answers, preferably on her terms. Chaotic break-ins were not her favorite event to attend.

"The likelihood that we will locate an Auranon with so much time elapsed is highly unlikely. Even spreading into the city would be a waste of resources. We are going to have to play his game, and when he re-emerges-which I'm sure he will- we must be prepared for him," Dromo gestured to the knights stationed guard throughout the throne room. "All we can do is double the guards throughout the castle and town in hopes that we will be ready. The unit being selected for the Western trip aside, most of our men will be posted here."

Haven's eyes sparked at the mentioning of the journey west. Dromo must have seen her face light up, for he ran a hand through his hair, slightly shaking his head.

"I was conversing with Aaren on the matter of the ride West," Haven started. Unconsciously she took several steps forward. "He acknowledged my strength in my fight with Aki, and he knows how well trained I am in the field of Knighthood. With his blessing, he said that I was allowed to join him on his trek. I hoped you might do the same, so that I can begin to prepare at once."

King Dromo shifted uncomfortably in his chair. "I was afraid of this."

Haven stopped. She looked up at him, and saw the uneasiness etched on his face. Her eyes fell as her voiced did. "You mean not to allow me to go, do you?"

"The world outside the Northern Kingdom's walls is a dangerous one, Haven. I lost your mother to that world and I certainly don't want to lose my only daughter as well." Dromo's posture was resigned.

Haven's mouth dropped open, incredulous. "Father, no more than a few seconds ago you just commended me on my actions in the study. I want to do this. It is my duty as princess of Eringoth to see that Aaren is reinstalled as king."

"Your duty as princess should be to practice your courtly etiquette, find a husband, and please our visitors. But that it not who you are," Dromo's voice suddenly filled the room; his hands gripped the arms of his throne. Haven suddenly felt very small. "You are a fighter, so I let you become a knight, despite every rule of tradition that stood in your way. In further pursuit of this path, I was going to ask you to fill Sir Gideon's position as Captain of the Guard in his absence. Do you wish to fill his place, or shall I place you into propriety classes once more?"

Haven was shocked into silence. In one moment, she wanted to scream that she wanted so much more than work the Captain's position, that it was she who had earned her knighthood, not because he let it be so. The next moment she wanted to throw herself to the ground and ask for forgiveness, for being a rude and ungrateful daughter. She did neither.

Haven looked at her hands. They were trembling. "What about my new gift?" she asked, taking off the white gloves so that her charred, blistered hands could be exposed. Holding them up so that Dromo could see, she continued. "Aaren said that he would mentor me in magic on the journey, so that I may overcome my fears and control it better."

Dromo eyed his daughter's hands and then looked away. "There are many sorcerers here who can help you with your powers."

"We both know that's not true," Haven snapped, her face flushing crimson. "I just spent hours begging for mages to mentor me, but every single one turned me out. I accomplish nothing by staying here, father. I can't discover my true potential if I'm walled in by such closed minds. I know I'm far from perfect- for the Goddess's sake I'm half human- but I want to see what I'm made of." She took in a ragged breath and added, "I need to."

Dromo's expression had closed off; his eyes darkened. Haven peered up at the king of Eringoth; her father had disappeared beneath the surface. "The Western Kingdom is on the perimeter of civilization," he started, his gaze and voice as cold as ice. "There are creatures and demons in those woods that we elves haven't named because they are so evil. I guarantee you there are men that we will see off tomorrow who will not return. If you were to go on this trek, I do not doubt that you will be able to hold out. But there will be death. And you will either survive and live on with the memories of those you lost, or you will be killed. Do you know what your mother said to me on her deathbed?"

The question struck Haven. She shook her head ever so slightly.

"She asked me to take care of you- to make sure that you never have to experience the trauma that she endured. Haven," Dromo's eyes became misty. "I would let Eringoth fall if I had to, if it meant ensuring your safety. But I have a kingdom yet to protect, and I need your help. Please. Take the Captain's position." By the end, Dromo's voice had fallen to its regular volume, but his entreating at the end made it seem all the more soft.

Haven was speechless. Her body was dormant; she couldn't even bring herself to look at her father. What was there to say? Dromo's words were chains around her ankles, and with each passing second she could see her future darkening. The journey was fading, her dreams crumpling like used pieces of paper.

Dromo rose slowly from his chair, treating Haven's silence as a submission to his request. He stepped airily down from the throne, translucent robes flowing about him. In a few lengthy strides he closed the gap between himself and Haven and encased her in an embrace. Haven felt herself return the hug, but it almost seemed as if she were watching herself from the outside looking in.

"You will make an excellent Captain," Dromo murmured over Haven's head. He stroked her long black hair with a gentle hand. "And you will do your kingdom proud, serving as the knight you were born to become."

Haven uttered a muffled thank-you to her father, her voice dead. Dromo must have known how hollow she felt. He had to have been able see the emptiness in her eyes when he pulled back and looked at her. He simply must have elected to ignore it.

The princess felt her voice leaving her mouth, asking if she may be excused.

Dromo acquiesced. "I love you, Haven." The three words rarely uttered by any elf bounced off of the bubble that had formed itself around her. She returned the three words, glancing at him with muted eyes before turning to leave.

Her footsteps resonated in the throne room, breaking the silence with every pace. She wanted to run and she wanted to collapse. Doing neither, she strode from the room with her chin sticking out.

When she left the doors and turned a corner, Haven stopped short to see Leonardo conversing animatedly with Aaren, one arm around the prince's shoulder. Aaren seemed to have been coming from the library; he had several spell books under his arm, books that he probably intended to show to Haven. In Leonardo's hands rested a little parcel- she had no idea what could possibly be inside but he seemed to be treating it with value.

Haven drew nearer to find that Leonardo was telling Aaren a story from his scholarly days. The grin on Aaren's face was wide and bright; he seemed to be immensely enjoying whatever Leonardo had to say. It was clear that they had just run into one another, and the two stepped along in an eager pace. They glowed with the pleasure of rediscovering their old friendship. Both were walking toward the throne room, as if they had intended to meet Haven there after she had finished talking with her father.

Leonardo saw Haven first, and his eyes lit up. "Hello there, lass! Prince Aaren here finally remembers that it was I who he kept a correspondence with back in University. Imagine that."

Aaren laughed, shrugging away from Leonardo. "I feel there is a traumatic reason as to why I had forgotten about you in the first place," he quipped. Haven had never seen him so lively.

When the two men approached her, Haven did the best she could to mask the heartbreak she felt inside.

Leonardo tousled Haven's head. "I'm more excited than ever about this journey, now. I have my long lost brother and my favorite lass along for the ride. This really will be a trip to remember. Here, I got you this to celebrate."

Leonardo handed Haven the package; she unfolded it to find a half-mangled piece of cake on the inside. She looked at it, a little confused.

"I dropped it on the way from the kitchens. But I know how you like pound cake," Leonardo explained, mildly embarrassed by the condition of the present.

"Thank you," she said absently, staring down at the crumbled cake. For some reason, it made her very sad.

Aaren picked up on Haven's mellow body language. He pushed onward, hesitating slightly. "King Dromo did confirm your spot in the party, correct?"

Leonardo eyed Haven with concern, his eyebrows pulling together.

Haven looked at the two men. Before she could say anything, tears began to brim in her eyes. "You're looking at Sir Gideon's replacement. I'm staying here, as Captain of the Guard."

Leonardo and Aaren simply stared. Apparently all three had simply assumed that Dromo would let Haven go on the quest.

Without hesitation, Leonardo swept Haven into a hug. "Haven, I'm so sorry," he was trying to piece everything together as he held her. "There's got to be a way. He has to let you go."

Haven struggled to keep herself together. She breathed deeply and said nothing, knowing that words would trigger an emotional response.

She was surprised to feel a second pair of arms wrap themselves around her. "I am going to make this right," Aaren whispered in her ear. Haven felt her heart skip a beat.

For a single moment, Haven felt that the two men around her were the only things that kept her from falling apart. There was warmth all around, and she could feel that the empty place in her chest was beginning to fill in. The moment ended too soon; Aaren had pulled away and stalked into the throne room, royal determination burning in his sapphire eyes. His navy hair disappeared from Haven's line of sight, and she was left to imagine just how that conversation would ensue. She could see his polite resolve masking over a very disgruntled prince.

Leonardo pulled back as well, assessing the condition of his friend. His leaf green eyes ached for her. "I had best take you upstairs to your chambers. It looks like you could use some rest."

Haven nodded silently. The two friends walked down the hallway together in the quiet. The evening light, blues and greys, began to choke out the sun, as it did every night. When they were walking up the stairs, Leonardo's hand found its way to Haven's. Grateful for the support, she let him lead her to her quarters. They stopped at her door, but Haven didn't unclasp her hand from his.

She inhaled, preparing to speak. "I'm going anyway."

Leonardo looked taken aback, eyebrows raised. He searched for the proper reply. "Haven, your father wants-"

"I know what my father wants," Haven cut in, looking up at Leonardo. He seemed almost intimidated by the resolve in her eyes. "But my country needs me. Out there. The role he gave me will merely be a formality, and no one here will respect my authority." The knight moved to speak, but Haven continued. "The people here have never taken me seriously. Do you believe that will change when my father forces more authority on me?"

Leonardo shook his head, understanding. "Perhaps Aaren can convince the king otherwise. He is quite the diplomat."

"No," Haven shook her head. "My father isn't going to budge. But I'm going to the West, even if that means I have to sneak out on my own to do it. These walls, my father- everything is holding me back." She exhaled loudly, swatting at tears that curled irritatingly down her cheeks. Her jaw was set. "Leonardo. I need to be free."

Leonardo squeezed her hand. He paused. "You're not going to be on your own. I'll do whatever I can to help, lass. After all, I am your knight." He looked sheepishly at her, but his mouth was set, too.

Haven swelled with gratitude, her mind already two steps ahead. The thought of liberation flushed her cheeks. "Meet me here later tonight after the watch, and bring Aaren, too. I have a feeling he'll want to be a part of this."

Leonardo nodded, a smile flickering across his face. "Our group will be complete with you in it. Together, we can take on the West and whatever comes next."

The princess thanked him again with a tight hug before disappearing into her room. The door closed and Leonardo lingered there for a moment, his hand in a fist, tempted to knock and bring her out again.

Moments passed. Leonardo let his hand drop and turned to leave, resolving to collect Aaren as soon as he was finished conversing with the king. He imagined that there would be a lot to plan in the coming hours. The knight retreated from the hall, his form fading until only echoing footsteps were left behind.

Haven strode across her room to stand on the open balcony. The moon was rising low and yellow in the sky, a sickly eye that regarded the land with a cross antipathy. Red clouds billowed in thick tendrils toward the castle, and lightning flickered in the curling mass of another storm.

The consequences for going against the king's orders would be dire, but her resolve was solid. It was time to strike out beyond the realm of the Northern Kingdom, and uncover the answers that lay like dormant giants in the hills beyond. Out past the mountains, a tyrant sat on a throne that did not belong to him, reigning with terror and dark magic that cloaked the land in chaos. And somewhere out there, a mysterious Auranon held a secret involving the death of her mother.

Haven gripped the railing and let the wind streak through her hair, inhaling the heavy air as if breathing fully for the first time.

The storm was coming. And she was ready.

To Be Continued…

Follow Haven, Leonardo, Aaren and Kohan in their next adventure.

SAFE HAVEN:
Warrior Chronicles
*Midsummer Tempest**

*Title subject to change.

MEET THE CHARACTERS:

HAVEN

LEONARDO

AAREN

KOHAN

DROMO

GIDEON

AKI

AND NOW, FOR AN EXCLUSIVE AUTHOR INTERVIEW...

When Andrews was just starting out middle school, she completed the first book of the Safe Haven series. Now that the story has gone through a reboot, let's see how the characters have reacted to the tremendous changes in their lives...

Caitlin: Welcome everyone! Today I have the honor of interviewing SH:WC's big stars: Haven, Leonardo, Aaren, and— wait, where's Kohan?

Haven: Running errands at the palace. Where else? You know how dedicated he is.

Leonardo: Yeah. He's so busy ruling be barely had any time to be in your book!

Caitlin: Oh, hush you. He has way more of a spotlight than in the first version. Aaren, why do you look so cross?

Aaren: ...

Leonardo: He's not responding. 'Cause that's not his name.

Caitlin: *sigh* I'm sorry guys, but I had to do it. I adapted both your original names from Christopher Paolini's book series- I didn't feel right using them here.

Haven: Hehe, just for the audience's sake, you should say their old names.

Caitlin: Oh, fine. Linduen and Arget, meaning wind and water respectively. I derived them from Paolini's list of spells in his first book, *Eragon*.

Aaren: Okay, I'm satisfied. Ask away.

Caitlin: So, Aaren, in the original book, your throne had been wrested from you seven years prior. How do you feel about this new shift?

Aaren: It definitely poses a more eminent threat. Not to mention it gives me a lot more mental problems.

Leonardo: You've always had problems.

Haven: That's funny, 'cause I remember you being the one to throw tantrums all the time in the good old days.

Leonardo: Ha! You're a pistol sometimes, Haven.

Haven: See what I mean!

Caitlin: Calm down with the shenanigans, you guys. This is a rented facility we're using for the interview. We can't have any chairs thrown across the room (at least without my say so). And besides, the anger only comes later, and it's because Leonardo was dying. Can you hold that against him?

Leonardo: I'm glad I'm not dying anymore. I like being alive much better. More things to eat.

Caitlin: How do you like being a scholar *and* a knight now?

Leonardo: I feel smarter.

Aaren: Pfft.

Haven: I think you're in the roasting seat.

Leonardo: Mm, roast. Now I'm hungry.

Caitlin: Aaaand moving on. Haven, originally you were intended to be twenty-seven years old. That number has changed since. How old to you feel now?

Haven: Last time I checked, I was twenty-three.

Aaren: From what I can recall, you acted more like a thirteen year old girl in the old story. Who has their first kiss at the age of twenty-seven?

Leonardo: Tsk tsk. You sad woman.

Haven: Hey--!

Caitlin: I take full responsibility for that one. Talk about pre-pubescent projection.

Haven: I hope my romantic life is a little better paced this time around.

Caitlin: Heh. That's for me to know and you to find out.

Aki: You mean, for *us* to know.

Haven: Aki! You said you couldn't make it.

Aki: I changed my mind.

Leonardo: Oh, great.

Aaren: Now it's a party.

Caitlin: Come now, guys, he does play a huge role in this book.

Aki: As I did in the last one. But now I have a question for the interviewer.

Caitlin: …Yes?

Aki: Why do I play such an antagonizing role? Previously I had helped Haven and her friends.

Leonardo: And you weren't even pleasant back then.

Caitlin: Ahem. To answer your question, Aki, I wanted to play up your dark side so that it could be contrasted with the good you do later. And you still helped Aaren in your first debut.

Aaren: He didn't have the greatest bedside manner.

Caitlin: But he is dynamic, which makes him fun to follow.

Aki: I'm still here you know.

Haven: Yes, you are Aki. Don't worry, I believe in you.

Aki: This isn't an intervention.

Caitlin: Aki's right. And sadly, it's actually time to wrap things up. I'm glad you could join us all for this special opportunity. Keep an eye out for the next adventure in the Warrior Chronicles. Say goodbye everyone!

Haven: I can't wait to strike out on my own!

Aaren: Salutations.

Leonardo: I hope this place has a salad bar. See you, everyone!

Aki: …*poof*.

Caitlin: Thank you for your support.

THE END

Made in the USA
Middletown, DE
09 September 2015